A Mind of Her Own

By Danielle Steel

A MIND OF HER OWN · FAR FROM HOME · NEVER SAY NEVER · TRIAL BY FIRE
TRIANGLE · JOY · RESURRECTION · ONLY THE BRAVE · NEVER TOO LATE
UPSIDE DOWN · THE BALL AT VERSAILLES · SECOND ACT · HAPPINESS · PALAZZO
THE WEDDING PLANNER · WORTHY OPPONENTS · WITHOUT A TRACE
THE WHITTIERS · THE HIGH NOTES · THE CHALLENGE · SUSPECTS · BEAUTIFUL
HIGH STAKES · INVISIBLE · FLYING ANGELS · THE BUTLER · COMPLICATIONS
NINE LIVES · FINDING ASHLEY · THE AFFAIR · NEIGHBORS · ALL THAT GLITTERS
ROYAL · DADDY'S GIRLS · THE WEDDING DRESS · THE NUMBERS GAME
MORAL COMPASS · SPY · CHILD'S PLAY · THE DARK SIDE · LOST AND FOUND
BLESSING IN DISGUISE · SILENT NIGHT · TURNING POINT · BEAUCHAMP HALL
IN HIS FATHER'S FOOTSTEPS · THE GOOD FIGHT · THE CAST · ACCIDENTAL HEROES
FALL FROM GRACE · PAST PERFECT · FAIRYTALE · THE RIGHT TIME · THE DUCHESS
AGAINST ALL ODDS · DANGEROUS GAMES · THE MISTRESS · THE AWARD
RUSHING WATERS · MAGIC · THE APARTMENT · PROPERTY OF A NOBLEWOMAN
BLUE · PRECIOUS GIFTS · UNDERCOVER · COUNTRY · PRODIGAL SON · PEGASUS
A PERFECT LIFE · POWER PLAY · WINNERS · FIRST SIGHT · UNTIL THE END OF TIME
THE SINS OF THE MOTHER · FRIENDS FOREVER · BETRAYAL · HOTEL VENDÔME
HAPPY BIRTHDAY · 44 CHARLES STREET · LEGACY · FAMILY TIES · BIG GIRL
SOUTHERN LIGHTS · MATTERS OF THE HEART · ONE DAY AT A TIME
A GOOD WOMAN · ROGUE · HONOR THYSELF · AMAZING GRACE · BUNGALOW 2
SISTERS · H.R.H. · COMING OUT · THE HOUSE · TOXIC BACHELORS · MIRACLE
IMPOSSIBLE · ECHOES · SECOND CHANCE · RANSOM · SAFE HARBOUR
JOHNNY ANGEL · DATING GAME · ANSWERED PRAYERS · SUNSET IN ST. TROPEZ
THE COTTAGE · THE KISS · LEAP OF FAITH · LONE EAGLE · JOURNEY
THE HOUSE ON HOPE STREET · THE WEDDING · IRRESISTIBLE FORCES
GRANNY DAN · BITTERSWEET · MIRROR IMAGE · THE KLONE AND I
THE LONG ROAD HOME · THE GHOST · SPECIAL DELIVERY · THE RANCH
SILENT HONOR · MALICE · FIVE DAYS IN PARIS · LIGHTNING · WINGS · THE GIFT
ACCIDENT · VANISHED · MIXED BLESSINGS · JEWELS · NO GREATER LOVE
HEARTBEAT · MESSAGE FROM NAM · DADDY · STAR · ZOYA · KALEIDOSCOPE
FINE THINGS · WANDERLUST · SECRETS · FAMILY ALBUM · FULL CIRCLE
CHANGES · THURSTON HOUSE · CROSSINGS · ONCE IN A LIFETIME
A PERFECT STRANGER · REMEMBRANCE · PALOMINO · LOVE: *POEMS*
THE RING · LOVING · TO LOVE AGAIN · SUMMER'S END · SEASON OF PASSION
THE PROMISE · NOW AND FOREVER · PASSION'S PROMISE · GOING HOME

Nonfiction

EXPECT A MIRACLE: *Quotations to Live and Love By*
PURE JOY: *The Dogs We Love*
A GIFT OF HOPE: *Helping the Homeless*
HIS BRIGHT LIGHT: *The Story of Nick Traina*

For Children

PRETTY MINNIE IN PARIS · PRETTY MINNIE IN HOLLYWOOD

DANIELLE STEEL

A Mind of Her Own

A Novel

Delacorte Press

New York

Copyright © 2025 by Danielle Steel

All rights reserved.

Published in the United States by Delacorte Press, an imprint of Random House, a division of Penguin Random House LLC, New York.

Delacorte Press is a registered trademark and the DP colophon is a trademark of Penguin Random House LLC.

Hardback ISBN 978-0-593-49870-5
Ebook ISBN 978-0-593-49871-2

Printed in the United States of America on acid-free paper

randomhousebooks.com

2 4 6 8 9 7 5 3 1

First Edition

To my darling children,
Beatie, Trevor, Todd,
Nick, Samantha, Victoria,
Vanessa, Maxx, and Zara,

May you always have the strength and
courage to stand for what you believe,
and may life be gentle and kind
and open the way for you to shine.

Wherever you are, whatever you do,
you have my faith in you,
and my love and support for who you are
and who you want to be.

I love you so much,
  Mom / d.s.

A Mind of Her Own

Chapter 1

Alexandra Victoria Peterson Bouvier was born in Paris in 1900, the last year of the reign of Queen Victoria of Great Britain. Alexandra's father was French, and her mother was American. The legendary British monarch had always had particular significance to Alexandra's American maternal grandparents, Paul and Miriam Peterson. They were born twenty-nine and thirty-one years after the famous queen, and had shared a great admiration for her, for her strength, her values, and the role model she represented for young, independent women.

Queen Victoria was eighteen when she ascended the throne, and she ruled an empire for sixty-three years. Both Miriam and Paul felt that she was a shining example of womanhood at its best. She ruled wisely and well, had been a devoted wife, and had nine children, who eventually sat on nearly every throne in Europe. She was both a modern woman and a traditionalist, and combined these traits effectively. Widowed at forty-two, bereft over the early death of her beloved consort, Prince Albert, she ruled alone thereafter. She was the longest reigning sovereign of her day. Paul and Miriam Peterson named their only child Victoria after the British queen.

Victoria Peterson, Alexandra's American mother, was born in Illinois in 1875, when Queen Victoria was still on the throne, and had been for nearly forty years. Victoria Peterson's dream for her daughter Alexandra was that she would be a strong, intelligent, independent woman one day, ready to take a stand for the causes she believed in, demonstrating her own ethics and the values she and her husband intended to instill in her. Alexandra matured exactly as her parents hoped she would.

Victoria Peterson had been born and grew up in Beardstown, Illinois, a town of just over six thousand people, two-hundred and thirty-two miles southwest of Chicago. Beardstown was an agricultural community, and Paul Peterson, her father, owned the local newspaper, *The Beardstown Courier.* He had lived in Beardstown all his life, and ventured out into the world to attend Princeton University, which opened his eyes and broadened his view of the world. He did a year of postgraduate studies at Oxford, took classes at the Sorbonne in Paris, returned to his hometown, and used the money his grandfather had left him to found the newspaper that became his passion. No matter how remote Beardstown was, or how distant from Chicago, he wanted to bring its citizens a deeper, more complex view of the world, and keep them fully informed of what was happening around the globe.

The Beardstown Courier was his pride and joy. It covered local, national, and international politics, world events, anything of major interest happening in Chicago, important agricultural news and innovative developments, and whatever widened the perspective of the locals, some of whom had never been as far as Chicago, and rarely left their farms. Paul Peterson made it possible for them to be up-to-date on a variety of subjects, no matter how small and remote their town was. He had a global mentality.

He had enjoyed his time at Oxford, and traveled around Europe when he was there. He had studied hard and returned to Beardstown nearly fluent in French and German. He had read their newspapers as well, and he had fallen in love with Italy. He had brought his exposure to other cultures home with him, and infused his newspaper with interesting information from abroad. He wrote a weekly editorial column on a variety of topics, and his newspaper flourished. People were hungry for what he shared.

Within a year of his return to Beardstown, he had a thriving newspaper, and married Miriam, the girl he had fallen in love with at seventeen, when she was fifteen. Her life experience was the exact opposite of Paul's. An only child of older parents, she had been sheltered and protected. Her father owned the largest dairy in the state, and she was educated at home, had never left Illinois, and didn't want to. She didn't even like Chicago. She was daunted by all the places that Paul had discovered and hoped to share with her. She preferred to listen to his stories about them, and read his editorials, rather than visit the places herself. She was well read and well informed, but her life experience was as limited as his was broad. He never succeeded in making a world traveler of her, but he loved and accepted her as she was. Paul's own family had a thirst for knowledge and education. His mother ran the local school. His father was an attorney, and both had shared their curiosity about foreign cultures with him. They focused all their attention and hopes on Paul, their only child.

Paul strongly believed that higher education was as important for women as it was for men. He wanted his daughter Victoria to go to a good university. Miriam didn't like the idea of her leaving home, but Paul convinced her that Victoria deserved to go at least as far as Chicago, and Miriam reluctantly agreed, to please him.

Victoria attended the University of Chicago, and was in the first class of women to be accepted in 1892. She was more like her father than her mother, and thrived on the experience of attending university in Chicago. She loved science the way her father loved journalism, and seriously considered becoming a doctor. She wasn't sure she wanted to invest as many years in medical school as she would have had to, and she let her mother convince her to become a nurse instead. She got her degree in 1896, and followed in her father's footsteps, doing graduate work in Europe. She attended Oxford, as her father had. Women weren't allowed to receive degrees or have full status as students at Oxford then, but they had been allowed to take classes there for the past twenty years.

Victoria thrived during the year she spent in England, and she followed it the next year by becoming one of the first women to attend the Sorbonne in 1897. She spent the year studying there, and learning to speak fluent French. Her parents loved reading her letters, and her reports of traveling in France with some other fellow female students. Her eyes had been opened to greater academic and cultural thrills than Beardstown could offer her, and she begged them to let her stay in France for another year. Her father was more than willing to allow it, but her mother balked. She missed her only daughter and wanted her to come home. She was afraid that she might meet someone and fall in love and never want to return to Beardstown. Paul assured his wife that it wouldn't happen, and that once she got the travel bug out of her system she would come home, as he had, and settle down. But in Victoria's case he was wrong, and Miriam's fears proved accurate.

Six months into her second year in France, having taken a job at a hospital in Paris, to help defray the costs of her lengthy stay and not wanting to be a burden on her parents, Victoria met Tristan Bouvier, a young doctor who practiced at the same hospital where she was working as a nurse, the Pitié-Salpêtrière. She was twenty-three years old and he was thirty. Within months they were deeply in love, and she had even less desire to return to the States. Victoria was happy in Paris, and loved living in Europe. Tristan came from a solid intellectual, upper-middle-class academic family. His grandfather had been a professor at the Sorbonne, and his father was a doctor too, and taught at the medical school. Tristan had plans to open his own medical office and start a private practice in the next year or two, and they talked about having Victoria work with him as his nurse. They had dreams and made plans, none of which included going back to Beardstown to work at the small rural hospital there. Victoria had seen too much of the world by then, and her mother had been right. It nearly broke Miriam's heart when she and Paul read Victoria's letter, saying that she wanted to stay in Paris, and that she and Tristan had just become engaged. It pained Paul to lose his daughter too, but a greater part of him was happy for her. She deserved more than their small agricultural community could offer her. And he couldn't think of a better place for her to test her wings than Paris. He just hoped that the young French doctor was worthy of her.

Paul and Miriam gave her their blessing, without meeting Tristan, and Victoria married him at Christmas, with their co-workers from the hospital and Tristan's parents and grandparents present, along with a few of their friends. The Bouviers provided a lovely reception at their home afterward. It wasn't the traditional wedding she would have had at home in Illinois, but it suited them. Victoria was sad that her parents didn't come for the wedding. But Miriam was in frail health—it was winter and she had a weak chest—and Paul didn't want to leave her alone, and she said the trip was too much for her. Victoria understood, and the Bouviers were lovely to her. They had a daughter now.

The young couple went to Venice for their honeymoon, and then came back to work at the hospital. It was 1898, and a year later their dream came true, and he opened his own medical practice in the 16th arrondissement, with money his father gave him to build his future. As he was an only child, his parents doted on him. It was a small office, but his practice grew with people in the neighborhood, and word of mouth. Tristan and Victoria were busy tending to their patients, and he did daily rounds at the hospital, to see the patients he admitted with more serious illnesses. Victoria ran his office impeccably. She was organized, intelligent, and efficient, and Tristan's patients loved her. Her nursing skills were excellent, and she had a warm, compassionate nature. She cared deeply about her patients.

Her parents kept promising to visit them, but Miriam developed a migraine every time Paul pressed her about it. She had fragile health, and was afraid she would be seasick on the boat getting there, or fall ill in Europe, or even die of some foreign disease. Paul was aching to visit Victoria and meet her husband and his family, but Miriam wasn't up to it. She cried for hours sometimes, afraid she would never see her daughter again. Understanding what was happening, and knowing her mother well, Victoria promised to come home to visit them as soon as she could. But there was never a good time to leave Tristan alone with his steadily growing medical practice. And months after he opened his practice, Victoria got pregnant, and Tristan didn't want her to make the trip to the States alone to see her parents. She promised to come to see them after the baby was born. Tristan would just have to find a relief nurse to take her place for the time it took. Victoria knew her mother wouldn't come to Europe and her father didn't want to leave her, or his newspaper.

Paul was tempted to make the trip before the baby came, to see his daughter and meet his son-in-law. But he worried about Miriam's health, and about leaving the paper for a month to make the trip. They had to be content with letters until the baby came and Victoria could come home to them. Victoria was diligent about writing to her parents frequently, and her father sent her copies of his editorial columns, which she had always loved. She missed their long conversations about foreign politics. She always learned so much from him.

Victoria assisted Tristan, seeing patients until the last month of her pregnancy, and then they hired a relief nurse to work with him. Victoria worked in the back office, handling the billing and bookkeeping for him until the last day. She'd had an easy pregnancy, and they were excited about the baby. His parents were ecstatic about their first grandchild. Victoria went into labor a few days before her due date, and everything went smoothly. She knew what to expect, and her arduous labor wasn't a surprise. The baby was delivered by a midwife with Tristan standing by. He held Victoria while the baby was delivered. The midwife let him cut the cord. Tristan handed their eight-pound baby girl to Victoria with a tender look and kissed her. Victoria was exhausted but triumphant after a long labor, and looked into the baby's eyes, wondering who she would be one day. Maybe she would be a doctor, like her father, as Victoria had wanted to be, before she became a nurse. A new era was dawning. Women were becoming educated, and wanted more in their lives than housework and children. Victoria's generation hungered for the opportunities that their mothers never had.

There was so much Victoria wanted to show her daughter and teach her. The old limitations were loosening their grip on women, and Tristan and Victoria wanted every possible advantage for their child. They named the baby Alexandra Victoria, and a month later, Victoria was back at work in Tristan's office. She brought the baby to work so she could nurse her, and they kept the relief nurse to help in the office when Victoria was busy with the baby, or seeing patients with Tristan. It seemed as though their number of patients had doubled. Tristan's patients liked him, and the energetic, youthful atmosphere that surrounded him and his wife.

Tristan stayed abreast of the latest treatments, and was innovative about new protocols and medications. Many of their patients were young, but older patients liked him too. He had a positive point of view about medicine and life.

As she had promised, Victoria took Alexandra home to visit her parents when the baby was six months old, and Tristan managed without her for a month. They had hired the second nurse as part of their staff by then, and a bookkeeper to handle the billing, so Victoria could spend more time with their patients.

Paul and Miriam were thrilled to see their daughter and granddaughter when they arrived. Victoria hadn't been home in four years. It seemed like an eternity. She was a wife and mother now. The crossing took a week, and Victoria spent two weeks with her parents. Her mother held the baby, and Victoria spent time at the newspaper with her father. It had grown impressively since Victoria left home. His newspaper was read by everyone in the area, and even by some people in Chicago, who loved his editorial column, and the broad scope and perspective on the news that he offered as daily fare. People who read *The Beardstown Courier* were well informed about world news, and the paper had won several awards for its presentation of international politics and events.

When they left to return home after a wonderful visit, Paul promised to visit them in France the following year, even if his wife didn't come. He and Victoria both knew that getting Miriam to Europe would be nearly impossible, with her health and her fears.

He kept his promise, and visited them in France when Alexandra was a year old. She was a chubby toddler then, with a mass of blond curls and big blue eyes, and Tristan and his father-in-law hit it off immediately. The trip brought back warm memories for Paul of his own time at the Sorbonne and the year he had spent in England before going home to marry Miriam and start his newspaper. Being in Paris with his daughter and son-in-law made him feel young again. They all had lunch together at Victoria and Tristan's home every day, before the couple went back to work seeing patients, and Paul took long walks around Paris, and visited all his old haunts. He even looked up two of the men he had gone to school with at the Sorbonne. One was a banker, and the other was working at his family firm, which made exquisite furniture. Paul bought a beautiful inlaid dressing table for Miriam and had it shipped home. He enjoyed meeting Tristan's parents and had lively conversations with them.

Tristan and Victoria were sorry to see Paul go when he left. It had been a wonderful trip. It had been complicated for him leaving the newspaper, but he had left it in competent hands. There had been no problems while he was gone. When they had urgent questions, they exchanged telegrams. But when he got home, he found Miriam unwell. She had been in bed, feeling weak and dizzy for most of the time he was gone. She hadn't told him in the letters she'd written to him while he was away. The doctor said it was her heart. She'd always had fragile health. Paul was worried about her, and wanted to take her to see a doctor in Chicago, but she felt too weak to make the trip. A week after he got home, Miriam had a massive heart attack and died. She was fifty-one years old and Paul was widowed at fifty-three. He had fallen in love with her at seventeen, and she was the only woman he had ever loved.

Victoria was devastated when she got the telegram from her father about her mother's death, and there was no way she could get home for the funeral. It broke her heart that her mother would never see her granddaughter grow up, and had only seen her once as an infant. Victoria hadn't seen her mother since her trip to Beardstown the year before. Her mother's health had deteriorated in that time. But even then, it had struck Victoria how much older her mother seemed than her mother-in-law, who was ten years older than Miriam. She was doubly glad she had gone home and seen her mother one last time, and she was sorry not to be able to be there to comfort her father when she died. Paul sounded strong in his letters, but Victoria knew how deeply he had loved Miriam and understood the immensity of the loss for him. She promised herself she would go home again in the coming months, but they were always busy. Tristan's medical practice continued to grow. She and his other nurse were constantly running. Their housekeeper took care of Alexandra every day, while her parents were at work, and they put her in school at three. Victoria taught Alexandra to read at four, and her father came to visit them again that year. It was 1904. He had been busy at the paper, and so had Victoria, helping Tristan. Paul stayed for a month and loved every minute of it.

Victoria took Alexandra to Illinois for a visit again when she was six. Tristan couldn't get away.

She took Alex to some of the farms, so she could see the colts and calves and lambs, and the child loved visiting the newspaper with her grandfather. Victoria was stunned by how big the paper had grown. The number of employees had tripled. Paul's mane of hair and beard were snow-white by then. He was fifty-eight years old, vital and energetic, as fascinated by the world as ever, and filled his life with his newspaper and missed his wife fiercely. Time flew too quickly, and it was years between their visits, but they were both busy, she with Tristan's practice, and he with the paper.

On the boat on the way back to France, Alexandra said she wanted to live in Illinois one day. She loved the miles of green fields, the animals, and the farms.

"I could work for Grampa at the newspaper. I want to be a writer when I grow up," she said with a determined look, and her mother smiled at her.

"And what will you write?" Victoria asked her. She and Tristan always encouraged her, although Victoria secretly hoped that Alexandra would be a doctor, like her father. It was what Victoria would have done, if she could. But she enjoyed her nursing too, and comforting people. She was a nurturer by nature.

"I'll write books," Alex said, smiling at her mother. "Grown-up books, without pictures in them." At six, she was bright and mature for her age, and her parents spoke to her like an adult.

"That sounds very interesting," Victoria said. "And what will the books be about?"

"I don't know yet," Alex said. "Grampa says that I can do anything I want to, when I grow up, if I work hard at it. I can be anything I want."

"He used to say that to me too," Victoria said with a nostalgic look. It was even more true now than it had been when she was a child. More women were going to universities, even more so in the States than in France. But it was happening everywhere. Some women were embarking on careers that had only been open to men before. Doors were slowly opening that had been closed to women. And by the time Alex grew up, maybe her grandfather was right and Alex would be able to do anything she wanted, be a lawyer or a doctor, or work at a newspaper. "Will you get married and have babies?" Victoria asked her, curious about what she'd respond. The days on the boat gave them time for lengthy conversations they normally didn't have in their busy lives in Paris when Victoria was working and Alex was in school.

"No, I don't think so. Or not till I'm very old. There are other things I want to do first," Alex said primly.

"Papa and I work, and we have you," her mother reminded her.

"That's true, you do," Alex said pensively. "Do I have to have children?" she asked innocently.

"No, you don't," Victoria said with a smile. "You don't have to do anything you don't want to. And just like Grampa said, you can be anything you want." She wanted to impress that on her early, to encourage her to follow her own path, as her own father had done with her.

"Maybe I'll work in the circus, and dance on the horses, *and* write books." Victoria smiled at her answer. Her father had taken Alex to the circus, and she had loved it. Despite her dream of becoming a writer, Alex was still a child. But they had encouraged all her dreams so far. She had wanted to be a firefighter the year before.

Alex loved the trip back to France on the boat, as Victoria wondered wistfully when she would see her father again. She hated leaving him, now that he was alone. He was only fifty-eight years old, but he seemed older now that her mother was gone. There was no one to take care of him, and he worked all the time. His newspaper ran like clockwork as a result. She'd noticed that whenever he wasn't working, he seemed sad. He still missed his wife acutely, five years after her death. He had no interest in other women, only work.

Despite her intentions to see him more often, Victoria only saw her father twice in the next eight years. He was busy and so were they. She had gone to Illinois once and he had visited them in France when Alex turned ten, in 1910.

Victoria was planning a trip to Illinois with Alex four years later, when war was declared in Europe, in August 1914, and it was no longer safe to travel. They canceled their trip. Neither her father nor Tristan wanted them crossing the Atlantic once the war began. France mobilized on August third and the plans for a trip to Illinois that month evaporated.

No one was surprised when Tristan volunteered to help organize and work a field hospital that was being set up to serve the front lines near the Marne in September, and Victoria enlisted to go with him. They needed doctors and nurses desperately.

Alexandra was fourteen then, and Victoria and Tristan had to make hasty arrangements for her before they left. Tristan's medical office closed in August, weeks after France entered the war, and both nurses enlisted in the army medical corps. Their patients were sad to see them go, and the Bouviers acted quickly.

The obvious place to leave Alex was with Tristan's widowed mother, Marie-Thérèse Bouvier, whom Alex called Mamie-Thérèse. Tristan's father had died of cancer the year before, and his mother was happy to have Alex come and stay with her, for however long the war lasted and her parents were at the front.

Alex was worried about her parents, and her father assured her that the field hospitals would be set far enough back from the front lines to be safe. They would be caring for the wounded men brought to them. He and her mother wouldn't be on the front lines of the battles themselves, which reassured her.

They said goodbye to Alex and Tristan's mother in early September, and left Paris on a gloriously sunny, warm day. Alex and her grandmother played cards after her parents left, to distract her, and they cooked dinner together that night. Mamie-Thérèse was a great cook. She was seventy-four years old, impeccably turned out, and looked younger than her age. She was full of energy and loved having her granddaughter with her.

Alex was a beautiful fourteen-year-old girl by then. She was passionate about writing and kept a journal. She still said she wanted to be a writer, she loved writing short stories, but she had a multitude of other interests, which her parents had encouraged, such as music and art. She knew a considerable amount about medicine from being around her parents, who talked about it all the time. But she had no desire to be a doctor or a nurse, even though she did well at science in school. She was a serious student and got good grades.

There was never any doubt that she would attend university one day. The only question was where. She thought she would enroll at the Sorbonne, but she was interested in England too, since her mother and grandfather had studied there. And with an American mother, her options were broader. And she spoke fluent English and French. Her parents had opened every door to her they could, and encouraged her to think widely of her choices and not to limit herself. She got along with her parents, and for now, she liked the idea of studying in Paris, close to home. But she wasn't entirely sure and was open to all the possibilities. All she wanted was for her parents to come home safely from the war.

When Mamie-Thérèse and Alex were cooking dinner on the day Victoria and Tristan left, they were still on the road to where the field hospital was being set up, near the battle of the Marne in

Saint-Gond. Victoria hated the idea of leaving Alex, but it was exciting too being part of the war effort, serving their country, and helping the wounded. Victoria could have stayed home in Paris with her mother-in-law and daughter, but she wanted to be with Tristan, and to make herself useful at the front. She wanted to share his work with him, and to serve her adopted country with him. It never even occurred to her to stay home.

She and Tristan talked on the way to their post, and she knew she would miss Alex, but they had important work to do, and they knew that her grandmother would take good care of her.

Alex was proud of what her parents were doing. All of her friends' mothers had stayed home to take care of their children, and Alex wished hers had too. But Victoria had explained that she had a mission, and a skill that was needed, as a nurse. Nothing could have stopped her from following Tristan to the front, despite the sacrifice it represented, and Alex was proud of her. She thought her parents were heroes.

As soon as the Bouviers arrived at the hospital, they could see how desperately needed they were. There were severely injured men on cots and litters everywhere in the tents of the makeshift hospital. Many of the men were unrecognizably damaged, some were moaning, others were crying, still others unconscious after surgery or in extremis. Two priests were wending their way between the beds, giving last rites.

Victoria and Tristan changed into their medical uniforms as soon as they arrived, and Victoria put on an apron and headed to the surgical ward where she was assigned. There were rows of men waiting for amputation. She didn't see Tristan again until

19

late that night. When she returned to the nurses' tent, she hadn't eaten, her apron was covered with blood, and she was almost staggering with fatigue by the time she saw him, waiting for her outside. He had had a long night too. And before they headed to their respective quarters in the tents reserved for the medical staff, he kissed her. By then, in Paris, Alex was sound asleep between the clean sheets in her grandmother's second bedroom, and Marie-Thérèse was asleep in her own room.

In Saint-Gond, Victoria lay down on the cot assigned to her, too exhausted to take off her clothes or her blood-soaked apron. She tried to force the horrors she had seen from her mind, and fell into a deep sleep immediately, with the smell of blood still in her nostrils. She was a million miles from their comfortable life in Paris, and all she could think of now were the men she was there to help.

The war had only just begun and there was so much for them to do. Victoria was certain that this was where she belonged, with her husband. The men she nursed would become her children for a brief time, and others would have to care for Alex while she was away. Victoria had more important things to do now. The wounded men needed her full attention, and all her experience and skill. There was no way she could stay home with one child now, safely in Paris. Her adopted country needed her. That was all Victoria needed to know. The boys she had seen that night were her priority, and Tristan's, and the field hospital was their entire world.

Victoria fell into a dreamless sleep, until a young nurse claimed the cot she was sleeping on, and Victoria stumbled to her feet to give it to her. She went to wash her face and change her clothes, and go back to the main tent, where hundreds of wounded boys were waiting for her, the doctors, and the other nurses. More ambulances were already arriving, with more damaged and dying men, as she ran to meet them with the others, to begin the day's work.

It was going to be a long day for all of them, and more wounded would be arriving, in a relentless wave of mortally injured boys and men, many of whom would have died by that night. It was the worst carnage Victoria had ever seen. She cried more than once before the day was over, and she fell into Tristan's arms with a sob when she saw him that night. There were no words to describe what they had both seen. The war was just beginning, and they could both guess there would be worse to come. They were seeing what war could do to human flesh, and the young soldiers they were treating were barely older than their daughter. They were observing firsthand what they all knew before, that war was senseless and cruel. And thousands of mothers and fathers, sweethearts and siblings, if not millions, would be grieving their lost boys and men before it was over.

Chapter 2

Alex was happy staying with her grandmother, although she missed her parents. They had little time to do so, but they both wrote short notes to her, which arrived haphazardly. Their letters took weeks to reach Paris, sometimes a month, and Alex loved getting them. She answered them with accounts of what she was doing. Marie-Thérèse did everything to keep her distracted and entertained and safe. But Alex was well aware of the fierce battles that were being fought, elsewhere in France, all over Europe, and in Russia. Trained by her father, Victoria read the newspapers every day, and Alex had learned to do so at an early age. She followed the war news diligently, and knew where the worst battles were. Marie-Thérèse tried not to dwell on it with her. By the end of the year, the field hospital had changed locations. They relocated to Ypres in October, to be closer to the battle to keep the Germans from reaching Calais. The fighting appeared to increase in intensity with each battle, the number of wounded greater, with the death toll rising.

Alex's parents came to Paris on a two-day pass at Christmas. It was a huge relief to see them. Tristan and Victoria had both lost a shocking amount of weight, working around the clock sometimes, with no time to eat, and rations that frequently gave them dysentery. Medicine was in short supply, and Tristan's mother could see in their eyes the tragedies they'd experienced at close range. Nothing consoled the medical staff for the senseless waste of life they were seeing. It made Victoria and Tristan more grateful than ever to spend two days with their family at Christmas.

They were shocked to notice how much more grown-up Alex looked. She had lost weight too, and her face was serious when she wasn't hugging and kissing them. She missed being able to confide in her mother. They had always been so close. Mamie-Thérèse knew she couldn't replace Victoria and didn't try, but she was a staunch support for her granddaughter, and a protector. She had no problems with Alexandra. She was well behaved and respectful and followed the rules. She had shown no great interest in boys so far, and spent all her spare time writing in her journal, or deep in a book. She enjoyed reading in both French and English. Victoria had taught her to speak English, and Alex spoke it with hardly a trace of a French accent. She was comfortable in both languages, and informed her grandmother of the war news she read in the newspapers. The news made Marie-Thérèse worry even more about her son. She was afraid that at some point the Germans would either bomb or overtake the field hospital where Tristan and Victoria were working, and take them prisoner. But she didn't share her worst fears with Alex, and maintained a cheerful outward appearance. On New Year's Day, they went to a restaurant for lunch, although rationing had impacted the quality of food all over France. The night before, Marie-Thérèse had opened a bottle of champagne, and given Alex a glass. She was almost fifteen, old enough to have a glass of wine.

Marie-Thérèse was conservative in most of her views, and a traditionalist. She didn't have Victoria and Tristan's advanced modern views about women, and she shared with Alex another view of the role of women in France in the past, to serve and obey their husbands with respect and tenderness. She had been deeply in love with her husband, married to him for more than forty years, and still missed him. She had taken care of him herself once he got sick, and held him in her arms when he took his last breath.

Marie-Thérèse admired some of her son's ideas, though not all of them, and she agreed that Alex should attend university when she finished her education with the nuns at a private girls' school in Paris. Alex was too bright not to go further. But Marie-Thérèse also worried that too much education might frighten off the men Alex might want to marry, and she didn't think a career was necessary. She accepted her daughter-in-law as the exception, admired her courage and independent spirit, and forgave her an excess of liberal ideas, because she was American. The American women she had read about always seemed particularly bold to her. Victoria never seemed offensive, but Marie-Thérèse tried to add some balance to Alex's upbringing while she was with her.

Her parents had allowed her to express her most independent views as freely as she wanted, and she occasionally shocked the nuns and the lay teachers at school.

Alex's American grandfather had written to her all about the demonstrations and parades of the National Women's Party in New York, whose goal was to obtain the vote for women. He thought it a worthy cause, even when the demonstrations occasionally turned violent. Alexandra and her mother agreed with him about the vote for women, and Alex voiced her opinions freely at school, and was sent home for the rest of the day by one of her teachers who found her point of view inappropriate, and revolutionary for a well-brought-up young girl. Alex thought women should be college-educated, allowed to vote, and hold any job a man could, for equal pay. She was far ahead of the few freedoms enjoyed by women in France, who lived in the Dark Ages, according to Alex. She assured her grandmother that no man would ever tell her what to do, which was why she had no desire to marry. She had no intention of becoming anyone's slave.

"That's a little extreme, don't you think, my dear?" her grandmother said gently, in the very polite, genteel way she had of speaking. She had strong ideas and opinions herself, even about politics, but she was never aggressive in the way she expressed them. Alex occasionally spoke too strongly when she was passionate about a subject.

"No, Mamie-Thérèse, I don't think my ideas are extreme. It's unacceptable to turn your wife into a puppet, and not let her have her own opinion."

"I wasn't a slave or a puppet to your grandfather. I took care of him because I loved him, and he loved me too."

"Didn't you ever want to have a job, Mamie, or go to university?" Alex asked, curious about her grandmother. Now that they were living together, she was getting to know her at a deeper, more adult level. Alex loved her, but she didn't agree with everything she said. And she thought some of her ideas old-fashioned, which wasn't surprising at her age.

Her grandmother considered the question for a moment before she answered. "I took some classes at the Sorbonne, while your father went to medical school. It was very interesting, and I might have enjoyed a longer education. I took a class in Italian literature of the eighteenth century. It was fascinating. But I never had a burning desire for a job. I wasn't brought up that way. And what work would I have done? I've never wanted to be a nurse like your mother. All that blood and dirt now. She thrives on that. And I wouldn't have wanted to be a doctor, if that were possible. I have no desire to be a teacher, and what else could I do? Work in a shop? I have no interest in that either. Women who work in shops always seem so envious and greedy. I was quite content to stay at home, take care of your father, run a beautiful home, and help your grandfather relax after a hard day at the hospital. And I believe he was quite satisfied with that too. He didn't expect more than that from me, and we loved and respected each other. He would have been amazed if I'd wanted a job. I didn't need to work. He took good care of me."

It was an interesting view of marriage for Alexandra, and very different from the relationship her parents shared. They were more equals than Tristan's parents had been. Marie-Thérèse wasn't seeking equality with her husband when she was married. And he protected her. She was quite content to be the tranquil haven he came home to at night after a hard day. That was her role, as she saw it, with occasional special moments. She had no desire or need for glory, or acclaim, and she preferred to stand behind her man, in her gentle bourgeois way.

Marie-Thérèse wondered at times if she was having any impact on Alex, and if she would remember her grandmother's ways in the future, and discover that her grandmother was wiser than Alex knew at fourteen. She was almost sure that Alex's mother wouldn't approve of what she was saying, but she thought Alex should know both sides of the story, the doctrine of the ardent feminists of the day on the one hand, which was familiar to Alex because of her mother, and the less familiar, subtler role of a traditional woman in France. Alex knew many of them, among her friends' mothers, aunts, and grandmothers, but she couldn't ask them the questions she could ask Mamie-Thérèse. Alex still couldn't see why she should want to hide in the shadows, and let her husband tell her what to think and do. Alex was much braver than that, and never wanted to be subservient to a man. If that were the case, she was sure she would prefer to be alone. She remembered her paternal grandfather, and he had always spoken to his wife as though he was smarter and knew better. He didn't want to hear what she had to say, and Alex didn't like it. It seemed demeaning to her. Her grandmother didn't seem to mind it, but Alex didn't want a marriage or relationship like that. She preferred her parents' more modern model.

"I don't want to marry," Alex informed her grandmother. "It seems too complicated to me."

"Your parents are happy and it's not complicated," Mamie-Thérèse reminded her, intrigued by her granddaughter's point of view, unusual for someone so young.

"They're different," Alex said, and Mamie-Thérèse didn't disagree with her. Her son and daughter-in-law were special. She had felt it from the first. They got along famously and viewed each other as equals, which was unheard of between a man and a woman.

Alexandra and Mamie-Thérèse had many discussions like it. And Alex's grandfather in Illinois wrote to her from time to time. He was very intelligent and more modern in his views than her grandmother, although they were of the same generation. Alex had only seen him a handful of times in her life. She had told him about the journal she wrote in faithfully, and he said he thought it was an excellent idea. And whatever their divergence of views and cultures, both her grandparents and parents were proud of her. She was allowed to speak her mind and she wasn't afraid to express her views, and had clear justifications for them that were coherent and lucid, even if Mamie-Thérèse didn't understand them all or concur. A wide range of opinions was acceptable in Alexandra's family, which was different from the girls she knew.

In April, at the front, the damage to the men Victoria and Tristan were seeing was worse than ever. The injuries were atrocious at the second battle of Ypres, where the Germans were using poison gas for the first time, with horrifying results for its victims. Many of them would never recover from the damage it inflicted. They were blinded and suffered agonizing internal injuries and horrendous deaths. In some cases, it seemed almost worse to Victoria when they survived, and death was a blessing. The doctors and nurses tried to save as many as they could, but the death toll was shocking. The condition of the men they treated demoralized the medical personnel as they made careful notes of what they were seeing in the men. And along with appalling injuries, the psychological consequences were intense.

Alex was fifteen by then, and noticed that her mother's letters were shorter and less frequent. She hadn't seen her in several months, since Christmas.

The entire world was shocked by the news of the sinking of the *Lusitania* in May, torpedoed by a German U-boat. One thousand nine hundred and fifty-nine passengers and crew were on board, and one thousand one hundred and ninety-eight lives were lost—British, French, American, and fifteen other nationalities. It was a civilian ship, and the Germans claimed that it was carrying military supplies, which the Americans denied. They had managed to stay neutral so far.

The photographs of dead children lying on the dock, retrieved from the waters of the Atlantic, were heartbreaking. Alex was deeply affected by them. Three weeks later, in June, her world caved in when she and Marie-Thérèse received the news of her mother's death from tuberculosis. Nothing had prepared her for it. She didn't even know her mother had been sick, her parents hadn't warned her. Tristan came home with her body in a simple pine casket. She had been ill for several months, and the doctors had been unable to save her. And she refused to leave the front, she wanted to be near her husband. Tristan was devastated, as was their daughter. When he was able to, once on leave, he had sent his father-in-law a telegram, who was equally crushed by the news. Victoria was forty years old, and her body was ravaged by the time she died. She was barely more than flesh and bones. Victoria had never mentioned being ill in her letters and had tried to sound cheerful for Alex's sake.

They buried her at Père Lachaise cemetery in Paris, at a simple service Marie-Thérèse arranged, and Tristan left for the front again three days later. He barely had time to comfort Alex, who was inconsolable. Her mother had been her hero, and the role model she tried to live up to. She worried even more about her father now. He looked tired and worn when he went back. It was a summer of deep grief for Alex as she mourned her mother, and there was little her grandmother could do to cheer her up.

The war news got steadily worse for the next several months. The Germans sank the SS *Arabic* in August, with Americans on board.

It was a grim Christmas for Alex, without her mother. Her father didn't come home on leave that year. After Christmas, the Battle of Verdun began in February, and the field hospital where he worked had relocated again. It was a bitter cold winter, and the men were suffering in the trenches. His world had become very dark when he lost his wife eight months before, and he hadn't recovered. His letters to Alex were short and infrequent. He had no good news to share with her. He felt dead himself.

Alex had her first flirtation that winter with a boy who was the brother of a girl she knew at school. It was innocent and chaste, and raised her spirits. It was the first thing that had made her happy since her mother's death. She had only seen her father a few times since. He didn't come home on leave anymore and worked all the time. Marie-Thérèse was worried about him too. His eyes looked vacant when she saw him, from too much anguish he was seeing at the front, with the continuing use of nerve gas and its devastating effects. The men who were surviving would be impaired forever physically and emotionally. It was the most vicious fighting the world had seen thus far in wartime, with cruelty beyond belief in an allegedly civilized world. Disease was rampant among those who weren't wounded— dysentery, typhus, tuberculosis. Men were dying from a multitude of causes the doctors had no resources to cure. Their medicinal supplies were limited to aspirin, quinine, arsenic, strychnine, and iodine, and were inadequate to combat the diseases they were up against. They had lost several nurses and some of the doctors too.

Julien Marceau, the boy that Alex liked, took her for walks in the Bois de Boulogne and the Jardins du Luxembourg. He was seventeen and Alex sixteen, and he was the first boy who had ever kissed her. He was serious and shy, and kind to her. His sister, Vivienne, Alex's classmate, joined them sometimes and they went out for ice cream. He visited Alex at her grandmother's apartment, and brought her small bouquets of flowers. He was polite and from a nice family, and seemed harmless to her grandmother. He was a sweet boy. He turned eighteen in August, and was drafted a month later, and sent to the Battle of the Somme after a brief training period. Before he left for the front in October, he told her he loved her. They had serious conversations about the meaning of life, and he was impressed that she intended to go to university. He was going to apply to Sciences Po after the war, an excellent school, and wanted to join the diplomatic corps one day. They had talked a lot about their plans and dreams, and everything they wanted to do after the war. He had never been to America, and wanted to go. She had told him about her grandfather in Illinois. She promised to write to Julien when he left, although letters to and from soldiers took a long time to arrive, weeks and sometimes months, and were erratic, like the letters from her father.

The Battle of the Somme had begun in July, and her father's field hospital moved there in August, to care for the relentless waves of injured men arriving daily and hourly from the battle lines. Alex knew her father was there, and she hoped that Julien would have no reason to meet him or need his medical services once he arrived.

It was only a week after Julien left that the dreaded telegram arrived from the War Department that Alex's father had been the victim of a bomb. One of his orderlies wrote to tell them that a German patrol had stealthily planted the bomb near the surgical ward where Tristan was operating. It had been placed by a spy in a French uniform, they deduced later. It killed six men—two doctors, three patients, and an orderly. Alex's father was one of the ill-fated surgeons. Three nurses had been injured in the blast, but none had died. It was counter to all the rules of warfare to attack a medical facility, but the damage was done. Tristan was buried locally—there were too many bodies to send home now. When Marie-Thérèse opened the telegram and learned of her son's death, she was as shattered as though the bomb that had killed him had hit her too. She had to compose herself to tell Alex the terrible news, and Alex let out a horrible wail of grief when her grandmother told her.

She took it as hard as Marie-Thérèse had feared. She sobbed all day on her bed, clinging to her grandmother until she fell asleep. And there wasn't even a funeral to honor him this time. The idea that she would never see him again left her breathless, and she began crying again as soon as she woke up the next morning. Marie-Thérèse was seriously worried about her, but there was nothing she could do for her, except be there. Alex had lost both her parents in the space of a year. All she had left was her grandmother, and a grandfather in America she hadn't seen in years, and barely knew.

She sat mournfully at breakfast, staring into space, unable to eat, as her breath caught in hiccups from crying.

"I'm an orphan now," she said in a broken voice. The look on her face brought tears to Marie-Thérèse's eyes again too.

"No, you're not," she said in a soft voice as she gently touched Alex's hand, "you have me." But it wasn't the same. Tristan was forty-eight when he was killed. She couldn't believe it either. She had lost her only child, and the only relative she had in the world now was Alex. She was seventy-six years old, and felt a hundred that day.

Marie-Thérèse took Alex out for a walk that afternoon, and they went to the nearby church to light candles for her parents, and Alex cried all the way home. She fell asleep on the couch when they got back, and Marie-Thérèse gently covered her with a blanket and let her sleep. Her every waking moment was an agony.

Alex didn't go to school for several days, until her grandmother finally insisted and walked her there herself. It was brutal getting through the days. Alex couldn't imagine how she would live without both her parents. They were more than her parents. They had been her best friends.

The days ticked by slowly, and the following week, Alex noticed that Julien's sister Vivienne wasn't in school, and she realized she hadn't seen her for several days. She was so distraught about her father that she hadn't noticed anything around her since the news of his death.

She asked one of their classmates in passing if Vivienne was sick. The girl shook her head.

"Her brother was killed at the Somme last week. She hasn't been back since. I visited her yesterday."

"Julien?" Alex asked in a whisper, and the girl nodded. Vivienne only had one brother, and he was it. He had only been gone for a few weeks. He hadn't even written to her yet. And now he was gone too. She walked straight out of the school, without speaking to anyone, and went home.

Marie-Thérèse was surprised to see her so early in the day. Alex was sheet white and stared at her when she walked in. She looked dazed.

"Are you all right?" her grandmother asked her. She looked like she was about to faint, she was close to it. It was one blow too many. Now Julien was gone too.

"Julien was killed last week, at the Somme," she said in a choked voice.

Marie-Thérèse shook her head, speechless for a minute, and began to cry as she took Alex in her arms and held her, as they both sobbed for Alex's first beau. It was a cruel way for the budding romance to end, and he was such a sweet boy, barely more than a child.

They sat down on the couch together, holding hands, and were silent for a long time, as Marie-Thérèse dabbed at her eyes with a handkerchief, and Alex stared straight ahead, as though seeing ghosts. She was still deathly pale.

Alex felt as though she was moving underwater for the weeks after her father's death. A month after he died, the Battle of the Somme was declared an Allied victory for the British and the French, with tremendous losses. And another month later, in December, the Battle of Verdun ended with enormous losses on both sides. It was hard to tell what was a victory and what was a defeat anymore. There were too many deaths at every battle. Alex wondered sometimes where her father's field hospital was now, but it didn't matter anymore. She had no one left to pray for or mourn.

Marie-Thérèse discreetly wrote Paul Peterson a letter to advise him of Tristan's death, in case he wanted to write to Alex, which he did immediately, listing all of her father's virtues and qualities, and saying how much he had admired him, and what a fine human being he was. It gave Alex some small comfort to hear from him, and she thanked him, but nothing dulled the pain, so soon after her father's death.

She and her grandmother didn't celebrate Christmas that year. There was nothing to celebrate. They went to church on Christmas Eve, came home, and went to bed. They ignored the holiday the next day, and treated it like an ordinary day. But nothing was ordinary anymore. Horror, heartbreak, and loss had become commonplace. She thought of Julien frequently too, and cried for him as well.

The war became increasingly brutal in the early months of 1917. U-boats sank Allied ships whenever possible. German submarines were combing the Atlantic for prey, even sinking passenger ships occasionally, though nothing as shocking as the *Lusitania* two years before.

In March, there was unrest in Russia, which ultimately led to revolution. The czar abdicated and his family were placed under house arrest in their palace.

China severed relations with Germany in March.

And in April, the United States declared war on Germany, followed by Cuba and Panama. All the European countries had entered the war three years before, but finally, despite President Wilson's attempts to remain neutral, at last America was in the war too. American troops were drafted, trained, and readied to be sent to the front in Europe. Brazil and Bolivia severed relations with Germany in April, and the Ottoman Empire severed relations with the United States and allied with Germany.

The battles were too numerous to keep track of, and Alex continued to read the newspaper carefully every day. Her mother had gotten her into the habit as a child and said it was important to be informed.

The Americans landed in France in June. The third battle of Ypres began a month later in July. China declared war on Germany in August. By the end of the year, all of South America had declared war on Germany. Alex's father had been gone for more than a year by then. The war had a viselike grip on everyone.

Alex had gotten a letter from Julien a year before, a month after his death. He'd written it the day he died. She cried when she read it. He told her he loved her and couldn't wait to see her again, and hoped that one day they could visit the United States together. The world as they knew it had continued to fall apart after that. Somewhere in the vicinity of seventeen million men and women had died by the end of 1917, among them three people Alex loved. And twenty million had been wounded.

She couldn't imagine ever being happy again. The whole world, and her world, had become a very sad place, with no end of the war in sight. Alex could not imagine the world ever being normal again. And her dreams had died with her parents and Julien.

Chapter 3

The weather in Paris was as gray as Alex felt in the early months of 1918. Her studies were to come to an end in June, she was almost finished with school. It was a rite of passage her grandmother wanted to celebrate, but Alex didn't want to acknowledge it. There was nothing she wanted to celebrate with both her parents dead. It seemed as though every doorway was draped in black. After nearly four years of war, everyone had lost someone. It wasn't a time for celebration. She hadn't applied to the Sorbonne yet. She planned to continue her studies, but she didn't know when. All the boys she'd ever known were in the army, and many of them were dead. The country was decimated, along with all of Europe.

People were tired and malnourished. They looked lackluster, skeletal, and pale. If they got sick, there were no medicines to cure them. Almost all the available medical supplies had been sent to the front for the sick and wounded.

In early March, there were rumors of a wave of influenza, which was believed to have started in Spain. Some said it started in the United States first. No one was sure. It spread to Germany and to France rapidly, and was commonly referred to as the Spanish flu, since it had supposedly originated there. It was said to be highly contagious, which proved to be true. Later in March, there had been a number of deaths from it, and the newspapers reported it as an epidemic that was rapidly spreading from country to country. The first official case in the United States was reported on March fourth, in Kansas, on a military base.

Alex wasn't worried about it, and didn't care if she caught it. Her life had been so grim since her father's death that dying of the flu would have seemed like a blessing. She awoke from her stupor and depression in mid-March when she heard her grandmother coughing late one night, and went to check on her. Her eyes were bright and her cheeks flushed, and when Alex touched her, her skin was blazing with fever.

"Are you all right, Mamie?" she asked her, worried. "Do you want me to call a doctor?" Alex felt a ripple of fear run up her spine. Marie-Thérèse didn't look her age, but she was seventy-eight years old.

"There are no doctors," she said in a raspy voice between fits of coughing. "They're all at the front, and in military hospitals," which Alex knew was true. "I'm fine." But she didn't look it. Alex made her a cup of tea with lemon and honey, and went back to bed with her door open, so she could hear her grandmother if she needed her or seemed worse.

Alex slept fitfully, waking every hour or so—she could hear her grandmother coughing for a long time, and then it stopped, and they both got some sleep. When she checked on her early in the morning, Marie-Thérèse seemed sicker. She went to the bathroom, holding onto the furniture as she went, and said she was dizzy and had a headache. They had some aspirin in their medical supplies and Alex gave it to her, but the fever didn't abate, and an hour later, she had a massive nosebleed that frightened them both. When it stopped, she fell asleep.

Alex was in and out of her room all day, but there was no noticeable improvement by nightfall or the next day. Alex had read warnings in the press that the Spanish flu was particularly dangerous for young people and the elderly. She didn't think of her grandmother as elderly, since she was so energetic and youthful for her age, but she hadn't looked well recently. Neither of them had, ever since Tristan's death. It had hit them both hard and demoralized them, but Alex had youth on her side. She didn't try to protect herself from her grandmother's flu. There was nothing she could do. The newspaper had said to wear a face covering in public, but hadn't suggested wearing one at home. And living together in close quarters, if she was going to catch it, she would. She had already been exposed.

By the third day, Marie-Thérèse couldn't get to the bathroom without Alex's help, and her cough was worse. Her fever remained the same.

Not knowing what else to do, Alex went to find a doctor whose office she had seen in the next street. She knocked on the door and a nurse let her in. She said the doctor was away and would be back in a week. Alex offered to take Marie-Thérèse to the hospital, but she said she didn't feel well enough to go.

"Should I get an ambulance, Mamie?" Alex asked her, feeling like a child again. She was scared. If her parents had been there, they would have known what to do, but Alex had no idea how to help her. None of the usual remedies were working to bring the fever down.

"Don't be silly. I don't need an ambulance, I'm not dying." Alex hoped it was true, but she looked awful, and she had two nosebleeds that day.

On the fourth day, Marie-Thérèse seemed confused, and mistook Alex for her mother, and asked her when Tristan was coming home from the office. Alex ran to the pharmacy then, and explained to the pharmacist what was happening. He confirmed that it sounded like the Spanish flu. He told her to be careful, wash her hands frequently, and not to touch her grandmother or kiss her, but she already had. She wasn't worried about herself, only Marie-Thérèse. The pharmacist confirmed that there was nothing she could do. She bought another bottle of aspirin, but it had had no effect so far, and it was the only medicine they had.

On the fifth day, Marie-Thérèse slept between coughing fits, and there was a rattle in her chest that Alex could hear plainly. She went back to the pharmacy, and he said it was almost certainly pneumonia. Marie-Thérèse hadn't eaten all day, and wouldn't drink the broth Alex warmed for her. She finally sipped a cup of tea, but she was rambling and vague, asked for Tristan again, and called Alex Victoria. She was clearly getting worse.

Alex wanted to take her to the hospital, but Marie-Thérèse wouldn't go. She felt too ill to go anywhere.

Alex sat up with her that night, and never slept. She watched her grandmother diligently, and she could almost see her fading away. After a particularly bad coughing fit, the rattle in her chest was markedly worse. Her breathing became labored then, and she slipped into unconsciousness as Alex watched in terror, sat next to her on the bed, and gently stroked her brow and her face, with tears running down her own cheeks.

"Mamie, don't leave me . . . please . . . you're all I have . . . I love you . . ." She gently kissed her cheek, as Marie-Thérèse gave a soft sigh, and exhaled her last breath. Alex sat staring at her, sobbing uncontrollably. She felt for a pulse and there was none. Her grandmother was dead.

Alex sat in the room with her for an hour, and knew what she had to do. She felt dazed and numb, as she put on a black dress and a black coat and walked to the embalmers that were a dozen blocks away. She told them what had happened, and filled out some papers. They had a doctor who worked with them, and they said he would come to fill out the death certificate when they took her away. The idea of her grandmother being taken away to be buried was terrifying. Alex had never felt so alone in her life.

She sat in the living room, and waited for the embalmers to arrive. They came in an hour, and she went to kiss her grandmother for the last time, and then they covered her and took her out on a litter carried by two men. The doctor signed the death certificate and gave Alex a copy. She was going to bury her grandmother at Père Lachaise with her mother. The mortician had told her that the new rule in the growing flu epidemic was that funeral services could last no longer than fifteen minutes and could be attended by no more than four people. Her grandmother was well liked, and had many friends, but there was no time to notify anyone, and she never thought to put a notice in the newspaper. It was all happening so quickly. Marie-Thérèse was to be buried the next day. It was like a nightmare from which Alex couldn't wake.

Alex sat up all that night in the empty apartment thinking about her grandmother. She had no idea what to do now. She didn't go to school. She didn't tell anyone what had happened, except the parish priest, who agreed to perform the brief service at the cemetery the next day. He would barely have time to say the prayer for the dead and then they would have to leave.

Alex wore a simple black dress and coat to go to the cemetery, and a black hat of her mother's that she had kept. The priest was there when she got to Père Lachaise. It was all over so quickly, there was no time for emotion. She had brought a bouquet of white roses with her, and left them next to the open grave, and she walked all the way back to the apartment in the gentle rain and was soaked when she got home. She stood in her grandmother's bedroom, and tried to think of what to do next. She knew where her grandmother kept a supply of money in a locked drawer. There was a woman who usually came to clean three times a week and do laundry, but she had been ill recently, and Alex wondered if she had the flu. There was no telling where Marie-Thérèse had caught it and it didn't matter now.

Alex went to the post office that afternoon and sent a message to her grandmother's lawyer, who was a family friend. He would know what to do. And she sent a telegram to her grandfather in Illinois, telling him of Marie-Thérèse's death. She thought he should know. He was her only living relative now.

The lawyer came to see her the next morning. She was surprised by what he said. Her grandmother had recently rewritten her will, after her son's death. She left everything to Alex. She had had some money, not a great deal, but enough for Alex to live on for some time. And a year before, Alex had inherited what her father had. Her grandmother had put it in an account for her. She was by no means wealthy, but she had enough to support herself when she went to university. Everything in the apartment was hers too. Marie-Thérèse had owned the apartment, which belonged to Alex now, so she had a place to live. But she felt lost as she looked at the attorney.

"What do I do now?" She felt like an abandoned child. She had lost everyone. She was alone in the world.

"Do you have anyone you can live with? Your grandmother never said. You can't stay here by yourself. You're the only relative I'm aware of," the lawyer said, feeling sorry for Alex. She was so young and looked so devastated.

"She was all I had," Alex said, fighting back tears, trying to be brave.

"You can't live alone in an apartment in a war. It's not safe," he said, concerned. But she had no other choice. "Do you go to school?" She nodded.

"I will finish in June." She didn't need to get a job, and she

47

had no skills at her age, and so few respectable jobs were open to women, except menial, domestic ones. "I was going to go to university, but I haven't applied yet." She looked lost as she said it.

"Perhaps you should stay at a women's residence, so you have some protection. Or hire a housekeeper to live with you, so you're not alone." She didn't like the suggestion. The apartment was her home, and it was too small for a live-in employee. These were the darkest days of her life. The lawyer promised to give it some thought, and said he would need her to sign some papers, to transfer her grandmother's bank accounts to Alex's name. It was a very simple estate, and Alex was the youngest client he'd ever had. She thanked him when he left, and made a cup of tea. She had hardly eaten since her grandmother got ill eight days before. It had all happened so quickly. She felt a chill as she drank the tea, and started coughing that night, just as Marie-Thérèse had.

By the next morning she had a fever and a pounding headache. She took one of the aspirin she'd bought and it gave her some relief. She climbed into her bed, and slept for several hours. She was shaking with chills when she woke up, and her teeth were chattering. She was sure she had the Spanish flu, and hoped she would die. She didn't want to live without her parents and grandmother. She didn't care about university anymore. She hadn't written in her journal in a week and didn't even know where it was. She went back to bed, expecting to be worse in the morning, but when she woke up, the fever was gone. She still had the headache, but it was better. Her throat was sore, but it was no worse than a bad cold, or a mild flu. And the next day, she felt fine. She was sure she'd caught the Spanish flu from her grandmother, but in her case, it was over in three days. Even though she was very thin and malnourished from the shortage of food, she was young and strong. She sent a message to her school then, explaining that her grandmother had died, and she had been ill herself, and would be back in classes the following week.

A long telegram from her grandfather arrived that afternoon. He was very decisive, took charge of the situation, and told her what to do.

He told her that she couldn't stay in Paris alone, that it wasn't safe for a young girl her age to be living on her own in a war-torn country. He advised her to put the apartment up for sale, or rent it if she could, and to get an estate agent to help her. Her attorney would know one. He said to bring all the things that had sentimental value to her, and to come as soon as she could to Illinois. There was more than enough room in his house for her. He said they would discuss her academic plans when she arrived. She was to get a certificate from her school, explaining what academic level she had achieved in France, and a summary of her grades for the past year. She was to take a ship to New York, and from there a train to Chicago, where he would meet her. He emphasized what he said by telling her that her mother would want her to stay with him, and not remain in France alone, and he was sure her father would too.

Her grandfather expressed his sympathy for the loss of her grandmother, who was a charming woman he had enjoyed meeting on his visits to Paris. He told her to be careful not to catch the dreaded flu, and to observe all recommended cautionary measures. He assured her that he was eager for her to arrive, and to advise him of what ship she would be taking, so he could tell her what train she should take, and make the reservation. He asked if she needed him to wire her some money in order to pay for her passage and live on in the meantime. He assured her that she would be safe once she got to Illinois, and he would take care of her. He touched on all the necessary arrangements in the same practical, straightforward way her mother had done when she was alive. He reminded her of her mother, which made her smile. But Alex was capable too. She looked around the apartment, after she read the telegram, wondering what she should take with her. She was going to follow his advice. There were so many of her grandmother's possessions that she loved. She and Marie-Thérèse had emptied her parents' apartment when her father died, but neither Victoria nor Tristan had been collectors of sentimental objects, and had put all their attention and funds on their medical practice.

There were three small paintings of her grandmother's that she loved, and a silver tea service that Marie-Thérèse used daily and which had belonged to her own grandmother. There were a number of things Alex wanted to keep, including her grandmother's jewelry. Marie-Thérèse hadn't had many pieces, but what she had was elegant and fine. And Alex had her mother's string of pearls and her wedding band, which was all the jewelry Victoria had.

Her mind was racing as she thought of everything she had to do. She sent a message to the attorney about an estate agent, and went to her school the next day, to ask for the certificate her grandfather had requested, and a list of her grades for the year so far. She told the headmistress what she was doing, and the woman assured Alex that they would give her the necessary files for her next school. She only had a few months to finish in an advanced curriculum and she was at the top of her class. She said goodbye to her friends, and they cried when they hugged. She didn't have many close friends. America seemed like it was part of another universe, and she wondered if she would ever see them again. It seemed unlikely, if she stayed in Illinois. She remembered how much Julien had wanted to go there one day, and now she was. She and his sister both cried when she left.

It took a week to pack everything she wanted in a dozen big boxes and two trunks. She asked one of her neighbors to store a small desk for her, and her grandmother's dressing table, and she authorized the estate agent to sell the rest. He said he would sell it at auction and wire her the money when it sold. He was going to rent the apartment for her, which would give her an income every month. And the lawyer promised to wire the rest of her money to a bank in Illinois when she arrived. Alex gave him her grandfather's name and address so he could contact her.

It took her three more weeks to organize everything and book passage on a ship. The SS *La Touraine* was still sailing to New York. It was one of the few ships still offering passenger service, and not being used for the war. She was well aware of the dangers, that the ship could be sunk by the Germans, but she wasn't afraid of dying now. If she did, it was her destiny. She wore a hat of her grandmother's as she left for the train that would take her to Bordeaux. The apartment was stripped by then. The auction house was picking up the furniture the next day, and there was nothing left that she wanted to keep. She had wired all the information to her grandfather, and he had made her a reservation on the train to Chicago. She had her school file in one of her trunks.

As she walked out the door, she realized it had been her birthday two days before, and she had forgotten it entirely in the rush of all she had to do. It meant nothing to her, with no one to celebrate it with her. She was eighteen now, an adult. She felt like one as she got into the carriage she had hired, with a truck to follow them, to take her to the station with all her boxes and trunks. Her grandfather had told her to book passage in first class. She had reserved the smallest cabin in Cabin Class, a new combination of first and second class. The ship carried one thousand and ninety passengers, had been entirely refurbished in 1902 after a fire, and had electric lighting throughout.

Alex got a last look at Paris, as the carriage rolled toward the Gare d'Austerlitz train station. She wasn't sad leaving the city, she was sad for the life and the people she had lost. She wondered if she would ever come back. She was leaving so much behind, the people she had lost, the life she had loved, the childhood that was so suddenly over now. She hadn't seen her grandfather for eight years, since before the war. She was a woman now, not a child.

The first part of the journey, on the train, took almost five hours, and the ship looked enormous to her when she saw it, with two funnels and four masts. It was specially equipped with stabilizers and was said to be unusually steady in rough seas, and very fast. She asked for the trunks to be sent to her cabin, and the boxes to go below. Her cabin was small but had a port-hole so she could look out at the sea. She went up on deck so she could watch as the ship set sail and left the dock.

She touched the hat she was wearing, and thought of her grandmother. She could feel Marie-Thérèse wishing her well, and sending her blessing with her. Alex was leaving the war be-hind and taking all of her memories with her, of her parents and her grandmother, and Julien. As the boat horn sounded and the ship left the dock, she closed her eyes and she could see their faces, etched into her memory and her heart forever, and when she opened them again, they were heading out to sea, to her new life. She wondered if the ship would be sunk by the Ger-mans or if they would reach New York safely. Whatever hap-pened, she was ready to face it. Without knowing, her parents had prepared her to be strong and independent, and she would have to be now, and very brave. She left her childhood behind her as they sailed away, and she was an adult.

Chapter 4

After they were well out to sea, and she could hardly see the distant outline of the shore, she went to her cabin to hang up her clothes for the trip. A maid and a steward were assigned to her, and offered to unpack her trunks, but she thanked them and said she'd do it herself. She had no fancy gowns to wear for the mandatory evening dress in the Cabin Class dining room. She had two sober black dresses of her own to wear, one of her mother's and one of her grandmother's. There were normally two sittings at every meal, but only one in wartime. There were previously more passengers, and some of the grander staterooms weren't in use. People made fewer crossings than they would in peacetime. No one crossed the Atlantic now unless they had an urgent reason to do so.

But in spite of the war, the SS *La Touraine* had an opulent interior and splendid grand staircase, an elegant dining saloon, and deluxe cabins in the modified Cabin Class. The ship had been very popular before the war, and was one of the few ships still sailing as a luxury passenger ship. She was extremely comfortable.

There were scheduled activities on board, and a swimming pool, which Alex intended to use. She liked to swim, and it had been a long time since she'd had the chance to. There was a card room, where men went to drink and smoke cigars, but it wasn't open to women. And there would be dancing on one or two nights in the middle of the trip. Some of the stewards formed the band during the war. Alex was listed simply on the passenger list as Miss Alexandra Bouvier. Her parents had always been diligent about keeping a current passport for her, in case her mother had to go to Illinois for an emergency and take Alex with her. Her passport was up-to-date, so she hadn't had that to worry about while getting ready for the trip. She didn't have dual nationality, since her mother had taken French citizenship when she married Tristan. But since France and America were allies in the war, she would have no problem entering the United States in New York. She noticed several American names on the passenger list, one of them a family of five. She hadn't noticed any young children on the deck when they set sail.

She had packed the only two formal dresses she had, and one of her grandmother's from before the war. It almost fit her, although Marie-Thérèse was taller than she was, but she had tried it, and if she tucked it up a bit under the belt, it worked. It was a pale gray satin and looked serious and elegant. Her grandmother had worn it to the opera when her husband was alive. And Alex would have to wear her own evening dresses more than once. She didn't have the wardrobe for a luxurious trip, but it mattered less during the war. No one was worried about their clothes, only their safety on the ship. They all knew what the risks were from German warships and U-boats they might encounter on the way. The captain had been artful at averting disaster before, and had a stellar reputation for speed as well as safety. Alex was well aware that travel by sea could be dangerous even in peacetime. It was almost exactly six years since the *Titanic* had sunk on her maiden voyage. But the risks were far more acute in wartime.

At five o'clock that afternoon, an hour after tea was served in the main saloon, there was a lifeboat drill and it was mandatory for all passengers to participate. There was a notice in Alex's cabin about it, with the number and location of her lifeboat station. It wasn't far from her room. She appeared in a long gray wool skirt to her ankles, and a beaver jacket of her grandmother's, wearing her life jacket over it as directed, and a black beret she used to wear to school. Her blond curls peeked out from under it, and she had pulled her hair back loosely, to avoid having it blow around in the brisk wind at sea.

There were about forty people already waiting at her lifeboat station when she arrived. Most of them were men traveling alone, and a few couples, one of them with two teenage girls who looked similar and were obviously sisters, and a tall young man in a suit and topcoat who was talking to the couple. He looked exactly like the older man, and was obviously their son, and she realized they were the family of five she had seen on the roster. They were assigned to the same lifeboat she was. Each lifeboat held fifty people. Most of the men were speaking French to each other, except for two Americans, and the family were speaking English, with an American accent. The two girls looked nervous, standing near the lifeboat, and Alex thought their mother was very pretty, with dark hair in a sleek bun, with an enormous hat and veil and a fur coat, although it was April. They were very well dressed, and the girls were well behaved. Their older brother noticed Alex as soon as she joined the group, and he smiled at her.

She looked serious during the brief drill, as they were told what to do if the alarm sounded. They were to make their way to their lifeboat station immediately, wearing their life jackets, as they were now. Everyone listened carefully, and were well aware of the dangers they could face on the journey. One of the young girls said she hoped they didn't hit an iceberg like the *Titanic*. The officer assigned to their station reassured her, and said that there would be none on the route they were taking, and that the *La Touraine* was a very sound ship. But they all knew there would be U-boats and didn't say it.

After the drill, Alex didn't linger to talk to the other passengers. She went directly back to her cabin to dress for dinner. She had brought her journal with her. She hadn't had time to write in it for weeks, and her entries had been sporadic since the death of her father. But she would have time during the trip, and intended to write daily again, as she had before.

She lay on her bed for half an hour, making an entry to describe the ship, and the lifeboat drill, and then she put it on the bed table, and ran a bath. The maid appeared at her door to offer assistance, and Alex said she was fine and didn't need help. The maid reminded her to ring the bell if she needed her, and Alex relaxed in the bath for a little while, thinking of all the changes that had occurred in her life in the past few weeks. She still couldn't believe that her grandmother was gone. It would have been fun to take the trip with her, instead of alone. Before the war, they had taken short trips together, to Rome and Venice, Madrid, the Alps in Switzerland, and London. They'd had a wonderful time seeing the sights and staying at good hotels, going to the theater and the opera and museums, exploring the cities they visited.

The ship had prided itself on its fine cuisine before the war, and had simplified the menus since the war began, but the food was still excellent. Alex's dress was black and very plain, and she had worn her mother's pearls with it. The simplicity of the gown enhanced her natural beauty, and several male heads turned when she walked into the room and sat down at her table. She was by far the youngest woman traveling.

Alex ate dinner at a table alone in the elegant dining saloon, and glanced at the other passengers, wondering who they were and why they were traveling. She saw the American family at a table on the other side of the room. They were laughing and talking, and it reminded her of her dinners with her parents before the war. It seemed like an eternity ago. It was hard to believe it was only four years since the war had begun. Everything in her life had changed.

After dinner, she took a walk on the deck, her hair flying in the breeze. She stood on the aft deck for a moment, watching the wake behind them. It was peaceful being on the ship and looking out to sea. There were blackout shades on all the portholes so as not to attract the attention of enemy ships. All the important art had been removed from the ship, to prevent its loss if the ship went down. Alex enjoyed standing alone in the dark, thinking. She felt peaceful for the first time in a long time. She hadn't been on a ship since her last trip to Illinois with her mother when she was six. After that, her grandfather had visited them. She barely remembered that trip now, twelve years ago. She had loved the trip and all the activities there were for children. She had gone to visit the kennel and played with the dogs. She didn't know if there were any on board now. She smiled thinking about it, remembering her mother.

She stood there for a long time, and then went back to her cabin, got ready for bed, and wrote in her journal. It was nice having this time and space between two worlds, her old life and her new one, without having to adjust to anything just yet. The boat trip gave her breathing space before she did. She was sure that life with her grandfather was going to be very different from her familiar cocoon with her grandmother. She had felt so safe there, and wondered if she ever would again.

She went swimming on the second day of the crossing, and afterward explored the boat some more. She had lunch in her cabin, and dinner at the same table in her other evening gown, which was pale pink satin and molded her figure. It made her look almost luminous and was more flattering than the sober black one she'd worn the night before. She noticed the American family watching her as she left the dining room, and she smiled.

The young man smiled back, and his sisters laughed at him. Alex stood at the railing on the darkened deck again after dinner, lost in thought, and was startled by a male voice behind her. She had been a million miles away, thinking of her parents.

"I'm sorry, I didn't mean to frighten you. My sisters and I were wondering if you'd like to play cards with us." When she turned around, he was smiling, it was the older son from the family of five. He was even more handsome close up, in a dinner jacket. He was tall, with dark hair and broad shoulders, and blue eyes. And neither of them realized it as they stood next to each other, but they made a handsome couple. They were a striking example of beautiful young people.

"That sounds very nice." She smiled at him. "I saw all of you at the lifeboat drill yesterday." And he had been watching her ever since.

"I saw you too. You're brave to be traveling alone." She had no other choice.

"It's not as scary as I thought it would be," she said honestly, and suddenly seemed very young. It made him want to protect her. "Everything seems very well organized . . . if . . . something happens." He nodded agreement.

"Are you going home? Do you live in New York?" he asked her. He had noticed the trace of a French accent, but barely.

"No . . . yes . . ." she said, confused for a moment. "I'm going to visit my grandfather in Illinois. I'm going to live with him," she added. "Do you live in Paris or the States?" she asked him.

"I've been in France for the last eight years. My father was the American ambassador to France. We were supposed to go home four years ago, but we kind of got stuck here once war broke out in Europe. So my father stayed for another tour of duty. They're finally bringing us home, and the Consul General at the embassy will be the acting ambassador. He's married to a Frenchwoman and has children there so he wanted to stay. My parents wanted to go home, at least until the war ends. My father's been reassigned to Washington." America had been in the war for exactly a year by then. "I've been exempted from military service because my father is a diplomat. I go to Yale," he said, as he stood at the rail next to her. She knew that Yale was an important university, and was impressed.

"That must be exciting."

"I like it a lot. My father went there too, and my grandfather."

"My grandfather went to Princeton. It's a shame that none of those schools take women. I would love to go to a school like that."

"Women have some pretty good options these days too," he said. "Barnard, Cornell, NYU, Penn. The University of Chicago takes women. I know two girls who go there. Are you planning to apply?" He liked talking to her, and she was obviously very bright.

"I am. I just don't know to where yet, or when. I have to talk to my grandfather about it."

"I'm Phillip Baxter, by the way," he smiled at her.

"Alexandra Bouvier."

"You speak amazing English," he complimented her.

"My mother was American," she said, and he noticed her past

tense immediately, and guessed it was why she was going to live with her grandfather.

They went to find his sisters and found them in the First Class lounge. They had two decks of cards and were waiting for his return. He introduced them to Alex as Georgia and Bethany, or Beth. The ambassador and his wife had retired by then, and the young people were entertaining themselves, and happy to have Alex join them. Georgia was a year younger than Alex, and Beth was sixteen, but looked considerably older. They were wearing beautiful gowns made for them in Paris. Georgia had dark hair like her brother, and Beth had red hair and green eyes. They were both in high school, and going to boarding school in the fall. They were looking forward to it. Phillip didn't mention it to Alex, but his father had presidential aspirations and he wanted to get to the States to get into the fray of candidates, before he missed his chance. Phillip was twenty-one, had political aspirations himself, and was going to be a senior at Yale in the fall.

Alex had a fun evening with them. The three Baxters teased each other mercilessly, and obviously got along, and Alex won three hands of gin. They played for a nickel a game and she won fifteen cents, amidst gales of laughter from the girls, and protests from their brother.

They invited her to join them for lunch the next day and they agreed to meet at the pool in the morning.

* * *

The following morning, the four of them swam until nearly lunchtime, and then went to dress for lunch. Phillip walked Alex back to her cabin.

"Thank you for putting up with my sisters. They get a little crazy sometimes." Beth had pushed Alex into the pool several times, but she was a willing victim and a good swimmer.

"I had fun with them," and she wasn't much older, but they seemed more carefree and exuberant. Alex was more subdued now than she had been before she lost her parents and grandmother.

"It's going to be weird living in the States again," he said to her. "I was thirteen when we moved to Paris." She knew he was twenty-one now, and he seemed very sophisticated for his age. "It's been nice having both, since I started Yale. And my father doesn't think he'll be reassigned until after the war. I hope he gets sent back to Europe."

"It's going to be strange for me too in Illinois. I haven't been there since I was six. I don't know when I'll come back to France."

"Are your parents still there?" he asked her gently. He had a feeling they weren't, from her reference to her mother the night before.

"No, they died in the war," she said quietly. "My mother three years ago, and my father a year and a half ago. My grandmother just died of the Spanish flu. So my mother's father invited me to come to Illinois. He owns a newspaper in a tiny town. I liked it there when I was a little kid. I don't know what it will be like now." Phillip nodded. The war had caused changes in everyone's life, but he was sorry about hers. He couldn't imagine losing his whole family.

"I'm sorry about your parents and grandmother."

"Me too. But I'm lucky I have somewhere to go. My grandfather thought it was too dangerous for me to stay in Paris alone, with the war on."

"He's right. My father was worried about my mother and the girls being there too. And now with the Spanish flu, although it's in the States now too."

"I caught it from my grandmother, but I only had it for a few days and it wasn't too bad. My grandmother got pneumonia from it, and it killed her in six days." Phillip looked serious as he listened to her.

"I'm glad I met you, Alex."

"Me too," she said with a smile. The trip was going to be a lot more fun because of the Baxters, having young people her age on board.

Lunch with Phillip and his sisters was lively and playful. Their parents were good-natured and warm. The ambassador was very dignified, and Phillip's mother was very kind to Alex. He had explained her circumstances to his parents before lunch, and they felt deep compassion for her, to have lost almost her entire family at such a young age.

After lunch, Alex spent the afternoon reading. She had taken an American novel out of the ship's library. She had dinner alone, and joined Phillip and his sisters again after dinner. Georgia was winning when an alarm sounded, and Alex tried to remember which of the alarms it was. Phillip's sisters looked instantly panicked.

"Is that lifeboat stations?" Alex asked Phillip, as she set down her cards.

"No, it's the alert, which means they've seen something though they aren't sure yet what it is, but we need to be ready for action once they know. We should probably change into warmer clothes," he said sensibly and calmly. All three girls were wearing evening gowns, which would be chilly and impractical if they had to get into the lifeboats. They headed rapidly toward their cabins, which were on the same deck as Alex's, and met the older Baxters on the way.

They regrouped on deck after they changed, and stood looking at the water and the horizon and saw nothing, and an hour later, the all-clear sounded. It had been unnerving, and the captain and crew were still watching the ocean closely. They had had a message from a British ship that they thought there was a U-boat in the area, but it never materialized.

Georgia and Beth went back to their cabin then, as it was late, and Phillip and Alex stayed on deck and sat in two deck chairs with blankets over them, talking. He was impressed by how calm she was. Unlike his sisters, she had never panicked. She'd been through a lot in the last few years, and kept a cool head in a crisis. And she had already made her peace with the possibility that the ship could be attacked and they might never make it to New York. She was philosophical about it, more so than he realized.

"You weren't scared at all," he commented.

"I was. But there's nothing we could do about it. If we're meant to get to New York, we will." She still couldn't envision her life in Illinois, it seemed so unreal to her. Suddenly she was starting a whole new life in another country. She couldn't quite get her mind around it.

"I hope I can see you sometime when we're both back in the States," he said. Alex was strikingly beautiful, and incredibly bright, and she seemed amazingly brave to him. "Do you think you'll ever come to New York? I could come down from Connecticut. Yale is in New Haven. Or you could come to Washington during school vacations—it's an interesting city." It sounded nice to her too, but probably unlikely.

"My grandfather never leaves his small town in Illinois. He's afraid some huge news story will happen and he'll miss it. And I don't know where I'll be going to college."

"Barnard at Columbia is an excellent women's college," he said and she nodded.

"I've read about it. My grandfather said we'd talk about my education. My mother and I stopped in New York on our way to Chicago, but I don't really remember it. I was more interested in the train then." She smiled and he looked at her in the dark, in the light of the moon. He wanted to kiss her, but he didn't want to shock her. They had just met the day before. But they had another five days of the trip left. He had never met anyone like her. She was so strong and direct, and gentle at the same time. She had very definite ideas about all the opportunities women should have, but she wasn't angry or bitter about the fact that they didn't, unlike some other girls he had met who were strident and even hostile about the liberties they wanted to fight for. He liked the way Alex presented her ideas, which was far more convincing than anger or insults. She just stated facts, and suggested ways it could be different.

They sat and talked for over an hour, and then he walked her back to her cabin. She slipped in quickly and didn't linger—she didn't want to start something she didn't know how to handle, and there had been no important boys in her life since Julien was killed at the Somme a year and a half before. She hadn't mentioned him to Phillip. It didn't seem appropriate. Telling him about her family was different. But Julien's death had affected her deeply too. For a brief time, she had imagined a future with him, it seemed so real, and then he was gone. It seemed as though everyone she loved died, and she took their ghosts with her wherever she went now. Phillip was so present and alive, traveling on the ship with her. He was three years older than she was, and seemed much more sophisticated than Julien had at seventeen. He was a schoolboy, and Phillip was more of a man, which made Alex more cautious with him. She was a well-brought-up young girl who had been protected, and she was fully aware that she wasn't worldly in the ways of men. They were a mystery to her. She had led a very sheltered life until then. She was intellectually mature and innocent at the same time, it was a very appealing combination.

Alex and Phillip spent time together every day. The morning swim with his sisters became a ritual, and was always fun. He induced his parents to invite her to at least one meal a day. On the third night, the most formal night of the trip, he danced with her, to the small orchestra formed by crew members, and she wore the pink dress of her mother's that made her even more beautiful and appealing, and look younger than she did in her other gowns, which were black and more serious.

Alex and Phillip went for long walks around the ship, and lay on deck chairs in the moonlight and talked for hours. There were three more alarms before the trip ended, which created considerable tension among the passengers. One night they had to get into the lifeboats and wait, while a submarine followed them, but it never attacked, and it seemed miraculous that they were spared. And on the last night before they docked in New York the next morning, Phillip got up the courage to kiss her. It was long and tender, and more searing than Julien's more innocent ones, and Alex felt a stirring within her. He was incredibly handsome and she was powerfully attracted to him, but she didn't see how their paths would cross again, with him at Yale and her in Beardstown. Maybe if she wound up at a college in New York, they could see each other again, but who could predict when that would be, or where their hearts and minds would be then. She knew that you couldn't count on anything during a war, and there was an unreal intensity to their emotions, hanging in space between two worlds for a week, whispering in the moonlight, flirting with danger, with death at their heels at any moment if the ship was attacked. Alex knew that if she fell in love she wanted it to be real, not illusion or fantasy. She wanted what her parents had had, a strong alliance of two like-minded people with the same goals, willing to risk their lives for what they believed in, while doing good for their fellow man. Her parents were her ideal of what she wanted to have and be one day. And her grandmother's more traditional views had affected her too. She kissed Phillip that night with tender feelings and growing passion, but she let it go no further and she didn't allow herself to be swept away on an unrealistic wave of hope for the future. She was a sensible young woman, not given to romantic illusions. And she had faced major losses at an early age, and was mature beyond her years.

They watched as the ship came into the harbor together on the last morning, and she cried when she saw the Statue of Liberty, with Phillip's arm around her, and he kissed her for a last time before they left each other to get ready to disembark. They stood in the same area on the dock, under a huge sign with the letter *B*, for both Bouvier and Baxter, as they waited for Customs and Immigration with all their belongings. Her grandfather had arranged for both a car and a truck to pick her up with her bags and boxes, and she was staying at the Hotel Martha Washington that night, a hotel for genteel women and businesswomen, where he knew she would be safe. Even the employees were women, so it was a safe place for the female guests.

Alex knew that Phillip was going back to New Haven that night to finish the term at Yale, after his spring break. And his parents and sisters were taking the train to Washington, D.C., to their new home there, a house the ambassador had rented in Georgetown, which they had yet to discover. Phillip's sisters were excited about it.

Alex's path and the Baxters' were about to go separate ways. She hoped she would see Phillip again. He had said that maybe he would come to Chicago one day, which was a five- or six-hour drive from Beardstown. The Baxters had made the trip a wonderful week for her, instead of a painful one, being slowly torn away from her homeland and everyone she had lost there. Instead, it was a warm experience, shared with good people, and a handsome and worthy young man who valued and respected her and believed he was falling in love with her. Alex sensed that it would take a huge effort to defy the geography involved and have a real relationship with him, but anything was possible, and time would tell what it had meant to both of them. In the meantime, she was grateful to him for the week they had spent together.

She hugged the girls before she left, exchanged a long warm look with Phillip, and waved as she drove away in the car her grandfather had sent, with the truck behind them, laden with all her possessions. The porters at the dock had put everything on the truck. She waved until they left the docks, and headed toward the downtown hotel on East Thirtieth Street between Park and Madison Avenues, in Murray Hill, where she had a reservation at the small, proper women's hotel. She had never been to a women's hotel before. It was a new experience for her. It was only noon by then and she had until three o'clock the next day to discover New York on her own. As she looked around, she could feel the electricity of the city, the horses, the carriages, the people, the cars and buses, the sounds of voices and horns. It was completely different from Paris, which was ancient and beautiful, and a symbol of previous history. Everything she saw in New York was modern and new, and different from anything she'd ever seen. She knew within minutes that she wanted to come back here one day. But for now, the car was at her disposal for the day, and she couldn't wait to explore the city. She had a day and night to do it, and was excited to get started, as she ran into the hotel to check in, and drop off all her trunks and boxes. They were going to keep them in a storage area for her until she left the next day.

She was back twenty minutes later, after checking into her very sober-looking room, decorated in dark green. She could imagine ancient dowagers staying there, which was usually the case, but she knew she would be safe. And she hopped back into the car and instructed the driver.

"Please show me everything I should see in one day," she said matter-of-factly, and the driver laughed.

"More like a week, or a month, miss."

"I only have one day and night. Please show me everything you can."

"Right," he said with a grin, and pulled away from the curb into the traffic with a honk of his horn, as Alex looked out the window with delight, and the sounds and sights of New York engulfed her as they headed uptown.

Chapter 5

Alex's tour of New York included every landmark the driver could think of that he thought she would enjoy. Tucked away hidden gardens, tall buildings, statues, views. They drove past beautiful homes and around Washington Square, and up Fifth Avenue. She walked into Saint Patrick's Cathedral to say a prayer and light candles for her parents, her grandmother, and Julien. The driver took her to two beautiful stores, where she bought a handbag, a silk blouse, and a pair of very stylish shoes that she wasn't sure would go over well in Beardstown, but she loved them and she had fun.

She went back to the hotel at the end of the day to change, and the driver took her to P.J. Clarke's for dinner, where they gave her a table at the back of the restaurant on her own. It was the first time she'd ever had a meal in a restaurant alone. The next morning he took her to a church in Brooklyn, where he said they had the best gospel choir in New York. It was the most exciting twenty-four hours of her life, and she made the train just in time, after lunch at the Grand Central Oyster Bar. It was an adventure from beginning to end. She gave her driver a very large tip with the fare for all his kindness to her, and he was touched, and told her to be sure and get in touch with him if she came back to New York. He wished her luck in Illinois. In the course of their day together she had told him she had lost her family to the war and the Spanish flu.

It took three porters to get all her boxes and trunks onto the train, and she settled into the compartment her grandfather had reserved for her on the 20th Century Limited. It was an overnight trip to Chicago, and there was a bed the porter would drop down for her. She remembered a compartment like it when she went to Illinois with her mother when she was six. But the 20th Century Limited was far more luxurious, and she was in awe of how her grandfather had spoiled her. It was an express passenger train. She had walked down a red carpet to board the train, where a conductor had handed her and all female passengers a bouquet of flowers and a bottle of perfume as a gift. The men got carnations for their lapels. The train had its own post office, barber shop, manicurists, masseuses, secretaries, typists, and stenographers for businessmen. It was pure luxury in every way.

Once she was in her compartment, she watched the countryside slide by during the afternoon, eventually becoming more wide-open spaces and farms. She had dinner in the dining car, and then went back to her compartment, wrote in her journal about the experience, and went to sleep. She felt like a baby being rocked by the movement of the train.

The conductor woke her at the time she had requested, so she could look presentable when her grandfather met her at La Salle Street Station in Chicago to take her home. She was excited to see him after so long. Her memory was a little vague after eight years, when he last visited them in Paris, when she was ten years old.

The train slowed as it entered the city, and followed a maze of tracks to the station, and at last they stopped. The trip had taken twenty hours from New York.

There were redcaps lined up along the platform, and she knew she would need several of them as she had in New York.

She'd had a quick early breakfast, and she was wearing her beret perched on her mane of blond curls, and a serious-looking black suit, as she stepped down from the train. She looked very French and she didn't see her grandfather at first. Then she saw a tall man peering at each car and the people getting off. He had changed very little, with his full head of snow-white hair, his broad shoulders, and long gait. When he saw her, he looked shocked as he hurried toward her and took her in his arms in a powerful hug. She clung to him, feeling like a child in his arms. He was the only family she had now. He was her whole world.

"You're all grown up," he said in a choked voice. He was stunned by how much she looked like her mother, but he didn't say it. He loved her for herself, not just because she was his late daughter's child. He thought she looked very stylish as they left the station, three porters following them with all of her belongings piled on their carts. He had driven to Chicago in his own car, and had one of the newspaper trucks, a driver, and extra men to follow them. They filled the truck with her boxes and trunks, and a little while later, they were ready to take off.

"Are you hungry?" he asked her, as they drove away from the station.

"No, thank you. I had breakfast on the train," she said politely. She felt faintly uncomfortable with him, after his exuberant greeting. She hadn't seen him in so long, and he had already done so much for her before she had even arrived. She thanked him profusely for the train and told him all about her day in New York, and he was delighted she'd had so much fun. He thought she richly deserved it after everything she'd been through. He wanted to make up to her for all her losses and the pain she'd had. It wasn't fair for someone so young to have suffered so much loss. He had had his own losses, both his daughter and his wife, but he was older and could withstand it. Alex was barely more than a child when she lost her parents, and now her grand-mother. But she was a strong young woman and had the resil-ience of youth.

The drive to Beardstown took almost six hours, with the news-paper truck following them. They stopped at one of the farms that had a small restaurant for sandwiches and tall glasses of cold milk. She felt out of place in her black suit and her beret. She was going to have to figure out what to wear, probably some of her old school clothes, although the skirts were too short now that she was grown-up. Respectable women's hems were worn a few inches above the ankle in Paris and no shorter. But she had no idea what women wore in rural Illinois. Her mother had always said that women in Chicago were stylish, as much so as they were in New York, but in the farmland around Beardstown, Alex had no idea what to wear, and she had no woman to advise her.

It was late afternoon when they got to her grandfather's house, and two men from his newspaper came to help unload the truck. They stacked the boxes in the hall so she could go through them when she wanted to, and set her trunks down in her bedroom.

Paul had put her in her mother's room, which was still beautiful years after she'd left. It was all done in pale pink silks, and was surprisingly sophisticated for a young girl. Their grandmother Miriam had decorated it with the inspiration of homes she'd seen in *Vogue* and Victoria had loved it. Her mother had made a beautiful home for them, which was still lovely now. Miriam had been gone for nearly twenty years, and Paul hadn't changed a thing in their home. Their bedroom still looked like a shrine to her, and her dressing gown was still on the back of the bathroom door, which Alex wasn't aware of as she settled into her room. She loved it, and Paul wanted her to be happy there.

There was a housekeeper who cooked dinner for them, chicken fresh from a neighboring farm, some early vegetables from his own garden, and apple pie for dessert, with homemade ice cream. There were orchards on his property that provided fruit in the spring and summer. There was land all around their home, with orchards, trees, and gardens. It was an idyllic setting. He told her some of the history of the town during dinner and she listened raptly.

After dinner, he looked at Alex and his eyes lit up.

"Do you want to come and see the paper?" He usually went back to his office after dinner, and stayed until they put the paper to bed. He had no reason to rush home at night since he lived alone. She knew from his letters how proud of the paper he was, and she readily agreed to see it with him. Her last memory of the paper was from when she was six years old on her last visit. And the memories were vague.

It was a short walk down the road to the building which housed the *Courier*. It was concealed by trees now, so she hadn't noticed it when she drove in. And as they drove behind the trees, she was shocked.

The Beardstown Courier was housed in a large building now. There were ramps where they loaded the papers into trucks. There was a row of them behind the building. When Alex stepped inside, it was all modern efficiency, state-of-the-art printing machines, the most up-to-date equipment. It was almost futuristic, it was so contemporary. Paul had bought the most efficient machines from anywhere in the world, and everything in the building was impeccable. There were still people in their offices, and the building was still teeming with activity, as they put the finishing touches on the paper. He grabbed a copy and handed it to Alex. She glanced at the front-page stories and saw that they were all interesting. He had a knack for choosing the right topics that fascinated his readers. She continued reading, engrossed in the stories, and he laughed.

"You can take it home if you like. Introductory offer, first one free," he said, and she laughed.

"You always pick such great stories to write, Grampa," she

said admiringly. He was truly talented at what he did. He made the paper exciting, and inspired people to want to read it. He was still writing his editorial column, which was a huge success, and got great reader reaction and comments. His newspaper was a jewel, and he nurtured it like a child.

"You can come and work for me this summer, if you like," he said warmly as they walked back to the house. "But first we need to talk about your plans for school," he said seriously. "Did you bring the information I asked you to get?"

"I did," she said, still impressed by what she'd seen. It was an impressive operation and had grown exponentially from what she remembered a dozen years before. The paper had been in operation for forty-five years.

Alex slept in her mother's childhood bed that night. It was an odd feeling, knowing that when she looked up at the molding on the ceiling, her mother had seen it too, long ago, and when she looked out the window in the morning, it was the same view her mother had seen every day when she got up, before she went to school. She felt as though she was following in her mother's footsteps in reverse. Her mother had left from here for her studies in Europe. And Alex had come here from Europe to have a new life, wherever it would lead her.

But school was the first step for her, and her grandfather got down to business after breakfast. He had already spoken to the headmistress of the local school, and the head of the school district. They were going to treat her as a casualty of war, a war orphan in fact. With the papers her grandfather had told her to bring with her, they were going to submit her to an exit exam on all the subjects they covered, in order to graduate. And if she passed the exam they would give her a diploma, which would allow her to attend college in the United States. She could go anywhere she wanted that accepted women. The choices were limited but some of the colleges that accepted women were excellent.

"I picked up the books they used this year in school for the high school seniors, so you can review what they've been doing. They'll administer the exam in a week. You don't have to go to class here, Alex. I'm sure you'll do fine at the exam, and get your diploma, and then you can decide where you want to apply for college." She was stunned by how much he had already done for her. He really was like her mother, who had been the most organized, productive person she knew. Her mother had learned it all from him. It was in her genes. Victoria's mother had never had that same energy—Victoria had inherited it all from her father, Paul, and Alex had it in her blood too. She just hadn't had a chance to use it yet, but Paul knew she would at the right time. He could see that she was an enterprising girl with a mind of her own.

She glanced at the schoolbooks he had picked up for her, when she went to bed that night. Two of them, science and geography, were almost identical to what she had studied in France that year. The history book was American, not French, which was unfamiliar to her. But in literature, she was far, far ahead. In addition, she had studied philosophy and had taken five years of Latin, was fluent in two languages, and spoke two more adequately. Math was not her strongest subject, but in her school in Paris, they were further advanced too. Her conclusion after looking through the books was that she had to work on her math skills and learn the American history, and the rest would be a piece of cake. Classes were more advanced in her French school. She reported that to her grandfather at breakfast, and he said he wasn't surprised. French schools had seemed more academic to him when he was there, and students went to school six days a week in France. The kids in Beardstown had to work on their farms too, and do hours of chores every day, and had less time to study.

He felt sure that Alex would do well at the exam. He took her to work with him that day, and she worked on the math problems in the book, refreshing her knowledge of algebra and geometry, and memorized some of the American history, about the American Revolution to free themselves of the British. And she studied the Constitution, which was the cornerstone of American government to the present.

She worked on it every day for the next week, and was ready for the exam at the local school. Her grandfather went with her the day she took it. The school was bigger than she expected. Several grades were grouped together in large rooms, with boys and girls together, of different ages. Many of the children on the farms were home-schooled. It was very different from her private girls' school in Paris, with both lay teachers and nuns. But this seemed friendlier and more relaxed.

They put Alex in a separate room on her own to take the exam.

Three teachers had created the exam for her on five different subjects, each with equal value to compute her grade. Three of them were essay questions. One was about the Constitution and what it meant, and the second asked how the history of a country affected how it functioned today. The last was an essay about the book she'd read that had affected her the most, and about herself. And there was a math section. The questions weren't easy.

She completed the whole exam in just under four hours and turned it in. She wasn't sure how she had done, because she was used to subjects being more academic and less subjective, but the topics they had chosen allowed her to express herself. She wasn't sure if she had gotten the math problems right. This was the same weak spot she'd had in France, but she had done her best. They promised to give her the results in a week, and her grade. Her grandfather gave her some jobs to do at the paper that kept her busy all week, and she forgot about the exam.

She had dinner with her grandfather at night, and they talked about interesting subjects. He told her that the Spanish flu was racing through the world and had become a pandemic, and was getting worse every day.

She still missed Mamie-Thérèse and sometimes she cried for her at night. Her grandfather was being so kind to her, and couldn't do enough for her, but it still wasn't the same. Mamie-Thérèse had been like a comfortable blanket that kept her warm. Her grandfather challenged her mind and made her think and stretch, which she enjoyed. And she liked working at the *Courier*. Paul had already told Alex that if she didn't pass the school exam, she would have to work with a tutor and take it again. She could get nowhere without a high school diploma, so for now that was her only goal.

The director of the school district called Paul at the *Courier* and asked them both to come in. Paul asked how Alex had done and the director said coolly that she preferred to discuss it in person. Paul was concerned that Alex hadn't done well, which surprised him because she was so intelligent, and adult to talk to. He was finding her to be great company in their nightly discussions. She was well-informed about current events in Europe, and well-read in the French classics, which weren't part of the exam.

Two days later, they met the headmistress and district supervisor at the school, in the head's office. They smiled when Paul and Alex walked in. They said she had the highest grade of any student in the school. She had scored ninety-eight overall in the exam and a hundred on the personal essay, which had everyone who read it in tears. They praised her for her writing. Her lowest grade was in math, an eighty-nine. Due to the circumstances of her arrival in Beardstown as a war orphan, and her academic excellence, they were giving her the diploma with Honorable Mention. They assured Paul that she would have no problem getting into any university with that exam result to add to her application, and her file of grades from France. And they said that with her history of why she was there, Alex would have the pick of any school she wanted that included women in their student body.

They shook hands all around, and Paul and Alex were both

beaming when they left the school. He looked at her when he put the truck in gear. "Now we have to get serious, Alex. You have to pick the colleges you want, and apply. We're a little late, but under the circumstances I think they'll give you a break on the timing. I have a list of schools for you to pick from."

"Near here?" she asked, looking worried. She had just gotten there, and wasn't ready to leave yet.

"Some are near here, and some aren't. Some colleges still won't accept women, which is stupid of them. We had the same problem for your mother. She loved the University of Chicago," he said noncommittally. He liked the idea of keeping her close to him now that she was here. He didn't want to lose her so soon, and she didn't want to lose him either. He was all she had now.

"She went to nursing school," Alex reminded him. "I want to study journalism." He looked pleased when she said it. "Then I can work for you."

"You can work for me anyway," he said gruffly, with a lump in his throat. He was very proud of her for the exam. She reminded him so much of her mother.

They got down to serious business that night after dinner. He had been researching appropriate schools ever since she arrived. He had wanted to see her first and get a sense of what she was capable of. In women's schools, he had Barnard College in New York City on his list, as well as Connecticut College, and St. Joseph's College for Women in Brooklyn, which had opened two years before. Rutgers University had just opened the New Jersey College for Women, and their first class would be open in the fall. Saint Clara's College in River Forest, Illinois, was well established, had existed for seventeen years, and was the closest.

Their other options were men's colleges that had become co-ed, which was an interesting possibility. Syracuse, Cornell, and the University of Pennsylvania, all great schools. And New York University had allowed two women to receive BA degrees in the last three years. The University of Chicago was the closest to what was now home, on that list.

"I really liked New York when I was there, Grampa, it's exciting," she said, her eyes dancing, and he frowned.

"You might want to save 'exciting' for after you graduate," he said seriously. "New York can be very distracting, and I'm not crazy about a young woman alone in New York at your age. It can be a dangerous city. Maybe you should save that for a job after you graduate and you're a little older. I'm sure you can handle it, but I'd worry about you." She nodded and wondered if he was right. Visiting for a day with a car and driver was different from living there, even in a dormitory.

They debated for several days, and finally settled on five schools to apply to. The University of Chicago, Saint Clara's College for its proximity, Barnard in New York, Cornell, and Syracuse. Each of them had advantages and disadvantages, and they decided to wait and see where she got accepted and narrow it down after that. Academically, Barnard was her first choice, and Paul agreed. She liked the idea of the University of Chicago because it was a good school, close enough to come home when she wanted to. Everyone seemed to love Chicago, and said it was a smaller, more manageable New York, and her mother had gone there.

She went to work at her grandfather's newspaper after that as an intern, helping out where she was needed. And a month later, she got the answers from the colleges she had applied to. Barnard said she had applied too late, and suggested that she wait a year and apply for the following year, which she didn't want to do. Cornell accepted her, and Syracuse put her on a waiting list. Saint Clara said their enrollment was full but they would love to have her next year. And the University of Chicago accepted her, which meant that the real yeses she had were from the University of Chicago and Cornell. She wasn't excited about Cornell, but she was about the University of Chicago. She accepted the day she got their answer. They had a department of journalism. Her grandfather said that if she didn't like it, she could always apply to Barnard for next year, since they had suggested it, and they had an important department of journalism. Privately, he was relieved that she wasn't going to New York. In his opinion, she was too young at eighteen to tackle New York. It would eat her alive. He was delighted with her choice of the University of Chicago. He could visit her there, and she could come home easily. And Alex was delighted too.

Things were moving fast in her life. She had been in Beardstown for six weeks, she had a summer job she loved at her grandfather's newspaper, and she was heading for college in Chicago in September. It was the best news she'd had in a long time, and she put her arms around her grandfather's neck, and kissed him. He hadn't been this happy since his wife and daughter were both alive. He was discovering that having a granddaughter was just as good. He enjoyed telling Alex about all the mischief her mother had gotten into when she was a little bit younger than Alex. Alex loved hearing the stories. It brought her mother alive for her again, and she loved having her girlhood bedroom.

The only cloud in the sky was that the Spanish flu was running rampant in the United States and Europe. It hadn't made it as far as Beardstown yet, but there were cases in Chicago. People were getting desperately sick and dying, while others only had mild cases, like Alex had had, but most cases were more like Marie-Thérèse had experienced, and thousands of people were dying.

Chapter 6

The summer sped by quickly, and Alex loved her job at the paper. Most of the tasks she performed were minor, but now and then someone gave her a bigger project and she really enjoyed it. She was friendly with everyone, and they liked her, even though she was the boss's granddaughter. No one seemed to hold it against her. They weren't jealous of her, and her tragic history before she arrived made them all feel compassionate toward her. She was the youngest employee at the paper, so there was no one her age to hang out with, but she didn't mind and loved her grandfather's company. He took her fishing, and they went swimming at a nearby lake and on little adventures. At night, they discussed world issues covered by the paper, and she wasn't afraid to argue with him if she didn't agree with his point of view. He admired that. Her mother had been that way too. He loved that Alex had a mind of her own and wasn't afraid to go toe to toe with him, politely. She was never rude or raised her voice to him, but she made her point, and stuck to it.

Paul invited her to write an editorial on women's right to vote, which was still being hotly debated. He thought the piece she wrote was excellent, and he published it. He wasn't afraid of opinions that differed from his own and thought it was what made life interesting.

The biggest story in newspapers around the world that summer was the Spanish flu racing around the world. By August, millions of people in every country had caught it and died from it, in a mere six months. There were no medications to treat it, nothing effective to prevent it. Face coverings were recommended in public by then, large gatherings were discouraged, touching, hugging, or kissing were nearly forbidden.

On Labor Day every year, Paul gave a big party with a buffet and barbecue in his garden, but he canceled it this year, afraid to make people sick, since the Spanish flu was so highly contagious. The symptoms were the same as any other flu, but stronger, and many people died of it.

One of the things Alex liked about being in Beardstown was that the war news didn't seem quite so ever-present. She saw the reports that came into the newspaper, and they printed them, but it seemed a little more remote reading about it in Illinois than living it in Paris with the fighting so near at hand. There were battles in the Marne again that summer, and in the Somme, where her father had been killed. Paris was under bombardment in August, which would have made life there unlivable.

In July, they'd had the tragic news that the czar and his family, still under house arrest, had been executed.

The war seemed to be going on forever, as was the pandemic. There was a severe outbreak of the Spanish flu in Boston over the summer, and Alex had received a notice from the University of Chicago that face coverings would be required in class. There seemed to be no stopping either the Germans or the Spanish flu.

On Labor Day weekend, Paul drove Alex to Chicago, and helped set her up in the dorm. She was sharing a room with a very nice Japanese American girl. She had been born in the States but both her parents were born in Japan, and they lived in San Francisco. Her father was an accountant. Her name was Yoko and she and Alex hit it off immediately. Yoko was very artistic. She was a biology student, with a minor in fine arts, and she wanted to go to medical school after she got her undergraduate degree. She did Japanese calligraphy in her spare time.

Paul was sad to leave Alex in Chicago, he was going to miss her, but it was nice to see her so happy. He gave her a big hug when he left. It reminded him of when his daughter started college.

The school was in the Hyde Park section of Chicago, in a safe neighborhood, and both girls made friends quickly. Alex wrote to her grandfather about the people she met, her classes and teachers, and he loved hearing about it.

As the Spanish flu gained strength like a hurricane, the war news improved, and at last the tides turned. As a result of intense fighting and the Hundred Days Offensive in France, Germany surrendered on November eleventh, 1918, and withdrew from Luxembourg and Belgium. The fighting ended in Africa, and in all the countries in Europe. It was over at last, and Americans were jubilant that their boys could come home. It had been a bitter war that had cost approximately twenty million lives.

Ten days after the war ended, Alex went home to her grandfather in Beardstown for Thanksgiving. He usually went to friends who invited him for Thanksgiving dinner, but they canceled due to the pandemic, and Paul was happy to stay home with Alex. They had much to be grateful for, and they had a quiet dinner together.

The entire nation was celebrating the end of the war. It had taken both parents from her, and Paul's daughter from him, but those who still had sons and husbands and loved ones abroad were jubilant. Plans were made to deploy the boys home for Christmas. It had been a four-year carnage for all the countries of Europe, and although the Americans had only come into it nineteen months before the end of the war, their losses had been heavy too. Paul and Alex talked that night about how senseless war was, and she hoped it would never happen again.

Her parents were heavy on her mind that night when she went to bed. She wished they had lived to see the war end. She was homesick and missed them, thinking about it, and Paul could see it on her face the next day. There were times when she was haunted by the heavy losses they had sustained, and probably always would be.

She had a letter from Phillip Baxter that day, the young man she had met on the crossing from France in April. He was back at Yale for his senior year. She'd had a postcard from him that summer, while he was on vacation in Maine at his grandparents' summer home. He said in his letter that he couldn't wait to graduate and get to work, and wondered where she was and if she had enrolled in college. He had no plans to come to the Midwest, but he hoped to see her in New York sometime. He was a sweet memory, but their paths didn't seem destined to cross anytime soon. She smiled as she read his letter, remembering when he had kissed her in the moonlight, sitting next to each other on the deck, and when they watched as the ship entered the New York Harbor and glided past the Statue of Liberty. It was so beautiful it had made her cry, and now the war was over. He had escaped it thanks to his father's diplomatic connections. It seemed unpatriotic to her, but maybe they were right in the end. He was still alive, and so many others weren't, like Julien, and millions of other men and women.

It seemed particularly cruel that now that the fighting was over, the pandemic was claiming millions more. It made her wonder when all the killing and dying would end. The peace they needed in their lives had been a long time coming.

She spent a peaceful weekend with her grandfather. They went for a long walk in the orchards. He seemed stronger and more vital than ever. He was excited that she would be working for him at the *Courier* again next summer, and he was thinking of having her write her own editorial column eventually, maybe once a month, about women's issues, and the problems that concerned young people that they felt no one was addressing. She could be the voice to speak for them.

Alex loved the idea, and could think of a number of important topics she wanted to write about. She was still deeply dedicated to the battle to obtain the vote for women. She believed in equality for all people, which Paul thought was a utopian ideal that wasn't realistic, but she was young and it was normal that she should be idealistic and have a vision of a perfect world to strive for, even if achieving it was just a dream.

"It will happen one day," he said to her quietly, as they walked back to the house on a crisp, cold day after Thanksgiving. "Not in my lifetime, but maybe in yours or your grandchildren's. The world is an imperfect, profoundly unequal place, and evening out those inequities is a life's work, and a noble cause worth pursuing."

"It's what you do with the *Courier*," she said, still deeply impressed by his ideals, and how eloquently he expressed them.

"No, what I do is different. I wake people up. I shine a spotlight on things and say, 'Hey, look up over here. Do you see this? Take a good look. What are you going to do about it?' I sound an alarm. And then it's up to them to solve it. I don't have the solutions. Most people don't want to hear those alarms. It scares them and it's too much work to fix the problem. But a few hear those alarm bells, and they care and try to do something about it. That's the best I can do, wake up the good ones and hope they fight to change it." Alex thought it was an interesting way to view what he did. She loved that he was a humble person.

"I think I want to be one of those people who change things," she said softly, thinking about it.

"Your mother was one of them too. The people who change things, who really make a difference in the world. So was your father. They were perfect for each other."

"I thought so too, but I was just a kid. We had so much fun together when I was little. They had fun, and made things fun for me." Her childhood had been warm and happy, thanks to her parents.

"That's important. People forget to have fun. They get bogged down in lives they don't care about and don't enjoy, and they get used to being miserable." He turned to look at Alex then with a serious look. "Don't ever get used to being unhappy, Alex. There's nothing noble about it. They don't give prizes for how unhappy you are. If you're unhappy, change it. Life is too short to waste it. We never know how long we have. We have to make every moment count, with good people and good ideas, by doing the right thing, and being brave enough to follow your heart and what you believe. Your parents did. They helped to set up that field hospital, and they loved helping people and saving lives. If you could ask them now, I'll bet they would say they have no regrets. They saved countless men and boys who would have died otherwise. I'm sure the only thing they'd regret is not being with you, but for the rest, it was what they felt they had to do."

"Sometimes I get mad at them for doing it, and leaving me.

They didn't have to," she said thoughtfully. "Mama could have stayed home with me and worked at the hospital in Paris, not at the front where she got sick because conditions were so bad it killed her."

"She couldn't have stayed in Paris," Paul said gently. "That wasn't who she was. She had to be there, with your father, at his side, helping to save all those boys. I always knew that about her—even as a child, she had to be at the center of things, doing all she could, giving everything, and once she met your father, she had to do it with him. It was who she was to her very core. It comforts me knowing that. She was where she wanted to be, doing what she loved to do. Maybe that will comfort you one day too." She nodded, thinking about it. Now that the war was over, they had time to think, and understand things better. She suspected that her grandfather was right. He knew his daughter well. She had to make a difference in the world, and she had, and Tristan with her.

"I hope I do something important one day, to make a difference," she said wistfully. She wanted to be like her parents, and her grandfather.

"You will," he said confidently, and smiled at her. "You can do anything you want, and be anything you want."

She laughed. "You told me that when I was six, when we visited you here. I still remember it. I told Mama and she said you told her that too."

"I'm glad you remember it," he said as they walked into the house to sit by the fire and get warm. "Don't ever forget it."

"I won't. I promise," she said, taking off her coat and hanging it on the hook at the back door of his comfortable house that was her home now too. "I love you, Grampa," she said softly.

"I love you too. You're the best gift your parents ever gave me. I'm sorry they had to die for you to wind up here."

"Yeah, me too, but I'm glad I came. Thank you for bringing me here from Paris. I feel like I was meant to be here, learning from you, and working at the *Courier*."

"You're going to be a fantastic writer one day," he said proudly.

"I hope so," she said, sounding unsure. They went to sit by the fire in his den, and a little while later, they went up to bed. He had said some important things that night, about her parents, about her, and about life. She hoped she would remember it all. She wrote down as much as she could recall in her journal that night. It had been a perfect Thanksgiving for them both, full of gratitude and hope.

When Alex went back to Chicago after Thanksgiving, she had two big term papers that she was working on for her final grades, and exams to prepare for. She loved her classes at the university, and most of her professors. She was almost always the only woman in her classes—in some subjects there were two or three, but they were definitely a minority, and at first it had taken real courage to speak up when she was asked a question. Some of the young men looked frankly annoyed to have to listen to a female point of view. But all of them reacted to her beauty. Some were intimidated by it, while others pursued it.

Two boys had invited her to study with them, which was a

bold move, and an obvious attempt to get closer to her. She was still shy, and felt uncomfortable being alone with a man without a chaperone. Many of the men were prejudiced about "overeducated women." She realized early on that it would take a strong, confident man not to be intimidated by a woman who attended university. She thought it a stupid prejudice, but there was nothing she could do about it. So she wrote an editorial on the subject in the *Courier* that brought in floods of mail. They were swamped. Their readers loved it. And her grandfather was immensely proud of her. Two female professors, who were her role models, congratulated Alex for her insight and the courage to speak up. It was the beginning of her editorial column.

There was a telephone in her dormitory, in the House Supervisor's office. It was for official use, but one of the younger supervisors let her use it occasionally, and Alexandra did to call her grandfather at the office. He had had telephones installed at the newspaper a few months before, and Alexandra loved to call him. She called him the week after Thanksgiving to thank him, and noticed while they were speaking that he had a raspy cough.

"Are you sick?" she asked him, worried. Even a cough could be a death knell at the moment, and despite his high energy and youthful looks, he was at a vulnerable age for the Spanish flu.

"No, it's nothing, I'm fine, it's just a cold. It's been freezing here since you left." She thought it had been ever since winter set in. She was shocked by the brutally low temperatures in Chicago and the surrounding area. It was never as cold in France, and it was bitter cold in the dorms in the morning. They kept wood stoves burning in their classrooms all day.

Paul sounded in good spirits during their conversation and didn't seem sick, in spite of his cold, and she put it out of her mind as she worked on her papers and did research in the library. She was startled when Josiah Webster, the managing editor of the paper, left her a message later that week. She called him back immediately, when she got the message at her dorm that evening. Use of the phone was unusual except for important calls. She called Josiah Webster back, and he hadn't left the office yet. Like her grandfather, she knew he often stayed late, and was incredibly dedicated. The two men had been friends since their boyhood.

"Is something wrong?" she asked him when he answered the phone on his desk.

"Probably not," he said to reassure her, "but your grandfather didn't come to the office today or yesterday. He says it's just a cold, but he never stays home. He comes to work in all weather and states of health. I was concerned and thought you should know. It's just as well he didn't come out. It's been snowing all day. He's got a nasty cough," Webster said ominously, and with the Spanish flu rampant, he wasn't wrong to be concerned.

"Do you think I should come home?" she asked him, instantly worried.

He hesitated before he answered. "I suppose not, not yet anyway. But I just wanted to advise you. I told him to call a doctor, but he never does. He thinks doctors are for old ladies, not for men." They both smiled at that. It was true. She would have liked to call him herself, but he hadn't had a telephone installed at home, only the office.

"Thank you, Mr. Webster. I'll talk to him at the office tomorrow, if he comes in."

"I told him not to, but he never listens to me either." But when she called Josiah the next day, her grandfather hadn't come in. She had worried about him all night, and her concern increased when she found him absent again, and she made a decision that night. She called Josiah Webster the next morning and asked him to send a car for her.

"It will take all day to get to you," he warned her. "We've had a lot of snow."

"It's all right, I'd rather come home to see that my grandfather eats and takes care of his cold." He agreed to send a car and one of the *Courier* employees. She wrote notes to the three professors she had classes with at the end of the week. She said she had to go home due to illness in the family. These days it was a valid excuse anywhere in the world, and had an ominous ring to it.

The driver the managing editor sent for her arrived at her dorm at seven-thirty that night. She sent him to a nearby pub to get a bowl of soup before they took off. The snowstorm hadn't hit Chicago yet, and he was back half an hour later, after a bowl of soup, a cup of coffee, and a shot of brandy to prepare him for the trip back, and she was ready to leave when he returned to the dorm to pick her up. She had worn her heaviest coat, a thick wool skirt, wool leggings and boots, a fur hat to keep her head warm, and wool gloves. She had brought only one small bag and her briefcase with the papers she was working on, and they set off to Beardstown. He had put gas in the car, enough to get them home.

Snow was falling when they were halfway there, but in small delicate flakes that didn't stick, and the wind had died down. They hit icy patches on the road occasionally, and the car skidded, but the driver was an expert at controlling vehicles in bad weather conditions, and had been driving a tractor and heavy farm equipment since he was twelve. Alex's grandfather had given her driving lessons the previous summer and she was a reasonably good novice driver, but she wouldn't have been equal to the task in heavy weather with ice on the road.

They arrived at Paul's home at three in the morning, tired and cold and blinded by watching the snow and keeping their eyes on the road. She thanked the driver, and carried her bags into the house. She left her coat in the front hall, and she could hear her grandfather coughing as she walked upstairs and stood outside his room, listening to him. She wondered if he was awake, and knocked softly on the door, in case he was. His voice called out immediately.

"Who is that?" She cautiously opened the door a few inches, and could see him in the distance, in his big bed, with the carved headboard. He recognized her immediately, and she couldn't see much from the doorway, but he sounded ill. "What are you doing here?" he asked in a sharp voice. "Don't come in," he said, stopping her, "I don't want you to catch my cold." Or anything worse, if that was the case. He wasn't sure. "Did you get kicked out of school?" he teased her, and coughed fiercely for a few minutes after he spoke.

"No, I have two papers due for school. I thought it would be more peaceful to write them here," she said quietly. His cough made her wince.

"You're a terrible liar," he responded when he stopped coughing. "Who called you? Webster? He's such an old woman. I'm fine."

"You don't sound it, Grampa," she said gently from a safe distance, glad that she had come.

"I'll be fine in a day or two. I get bronchitis every winter, it won't kill me. Now go to bed, so you don't catch a cold yourself. I'll see you in the morning." He sounded gruff, but he was weak and ill. And secretly, he was happy to see her.

She closed the door softly and went to her own room, which was bitter cold, since no one knew she was coming and they hadn't lit the fire. She lit it herself, with the kindling and logs neatly stacked next to the fireplace, and got ready for bed. She lay thinking about her grandfather, wondering if she should call the doctor herself in the morning. Her grandfather would have a fit, but she thought he needed one, to make sure he didn't have pneumonia. She fell asleep, dreaming of Mamie. She didn't want anything like that to happen to Paul.

Her grandfather's lawyer arrived the next morning while Alex was having breakfast and pondering whether to call the doctor or not.

She didn't interrupt while the lawyer was there. It was so like her grandfather to go on conducting business from bed, while he was sick. He hated giving in to illness. And when she saw him after the lawyer left two hours later, it was an easy decision for her. He was sheet white, with two bright scarlet spots on his cheeks from the fever. But he sounded strong and in control, despite the deep cough.

She sent the housekeeper to the office to call the doctor and he came before lunch, and reassured Alex that Paul didn't have pneumonia.

"Is it bronchitis?"

The doctor looked grim and shook his head. "He has all the symptoms of Spanish flu, including the loss of his sense of smell. But he's a strong man and in good health. He should come through it." Alex was praying he would. He was younger than Marie-Thérèse had been, and in much better health than anyone in France after years of starvation and war. "Call me if anything changes," the doctor said before he left.

Alex only saw her grandfather from the doorway, wearing a face mask so as not to catch it again, if that was possible, which no one knew for sure. She was encouraged to see him looking better, although he was perspiring from the fever and his hair was damp.

He ate very little for lunch when she checked, and he slept all afternoon. When she stood in the doorway again at dinnertime, the red cheeks were gone, and he looked uniformly pale and sounded much weaker than he had only hours before. She'd been hoping that sleep would cure him but it didn't, and his cough was the same.

Alex stayed up all night, and listened at his door at regular intervals, but nothing seemed different. The cough was ugly, but no worse. The room got quieter as the sun came up, and she went to her room to get some sleep herself for a few hours. Paul was with his lawyer again when she woke. She wore her mask and walked into the room where he was at his desk signing papers, and she scolded him. His attorney was wearing a mask too, as was Paul, not to spread germs. She knew the papers must be important if his lawyer was there again, and willing to risk Spanish flu. They had been friends for years, and the attorney looked distressed when he left.

Paul looked exhausted when he got back to bed after his lawyer left, and Alex wanted to sit quietly next to him, but he wouldn't let her. He told her to go and work on her two papers, or study something so her grades wouldn't slip. They never had before, even in France, with much worse things happening, although her grandfather having the Spanish flu was pretty bad. She was frightened.

He refused dinner that night, and when she checked on him at midnight, he was rambling and imagined he was talking to his wife about their daughter Victoria staying in Europe to work longer in Paris. He was arguing with his wife on her behalf, as he had then.

Alex retreated to a chair in the far corner of the room where he couldn't see her, and he was too delirious to notice, but she wanted to watch him through the night. He fell asleep finally, coughing in his sleep, and she sent for the doctor the next morning before he woke up. The doctor confirmed her fears immediately when he listened to Paul's chest, while he was still asleep. He had pneumonia. All the doctor could suggest was aspirin. He said that the poisons some people had tried, arsenic and strychnine, would do him no good, and might kill him. And the nearest hospital was too far away to risk the journey in freezing weather. They had no magic remedies for the flu either. All they could do was wait.

Paul didn't wake until that afternoon, and only briefly. Alex had a vise on her heart as she watched him. She had seen this scene nine months before with her grandmother.

That evening, he woke up and seemed coherent at last. He recognized Alex immediately, thanked her for taking care of him, and his voice sounded stronger. He sat up in bed and drank a mug of broth. He lamented all the news he was missing and he said he'd write his editorial in the morning. He was engaged in life again and she thought he was better. She continued her vigil that night, oblivious to the risk to herself. She didn't want to leave him alone. And at midnight she heard the same rattle in his chest she had heard with Marie-Thérèse, and the labored breathing that followed. He was asleep, and didn't wake up, as she sat closer to him to watch him. And an hour later there was no sound at all. He lay perfectly still and looked peaceful, as Alex stared at him with rivers of tears running down her cheeks. Her last relative on earth, her beloved grandfather, was dead.

Chapter 7

The undertakers took Paul Peterson's body from his home the morning he died. Alex sat with him for a little while before they came, with the terrible déjà vu of her grandmother's death. She didn't know her grandfather as well, but she loved him and had come to know him better since she arrived eight months before. She'd had a chance to hear his philosophies of life, and enjoy his company after she came to live with him. It made his passing all the more painful for her. At eighteen, she had lost everyone she had ever loved, due to the war, her mother's illness as a result, and the Spanish flu.

The ground was too frozen for him to be buried, so the undertakers would keep his body until the weather allowed them to put him in the ground, at the family plot in the Beardstown cemetery. He would be buried next to his wife, and near his parents. There was a small memorial marker for his daughter and son-in-law, who were buried in France.

Following the rules born of the pandemic, only ten people were allowed to attend the church service at the local Presbyterian church, which he hadn't attended in years, though the minister knew him well. Miriam had been a member of the congregation but Paul never had been. Paul had as little interest in religion as he did in medicine, for himself. He was a down-to-earth realist and pragmatist, who was actively engaged in the present, with no thought of the afterlife. Alex had been baptized Catholic because her father was, but her father was no more interested in religion than her grandfather was. Tristan believed in science, and Paul believed in life on earth, good men and bad men, and being honorable and honest while you were alive. Victoria was more religious than her husband and father, and had shared her faith with her daughter, so Alex took some comfort in praying for all the family members she had lost. She and Marie-Thérèse had gone to church often. Alex had a full range of beliefs to choose from, which helped her now.

The managing editor of the newspaper, Josiah Webster, was one of the ten people at the church service, and so was Paul's lawyer and boyhood friend, who had been one of the last people to see him. His housekeeper, Alice, who had been loyal to him and Miriam for years, the assistant publisher of the *Courier*, Alex, his only grandchild, and five men who had been his friends since his school days and still lived in Beardstown were there too. In normal times, nearly the entire town would have attended Paul's funeral, too many to fit in the church, with people who had come from Chicago who knew and respected him, but that was no longer possible in the face of the pandemic. The handful of people sitting spaced apart in the church all wore masks, as did the minister. Paul had considered cremation, but thought it would upset his granddaughter because she was Catholic, so in deference to her, he had decided against it. Cremation was forbidden by the Catholic church. He had no thoughts about heaven or hell or purgatory, or what would come next. He was only interested in the people he loved while he was with them on earth, and providing for them as best he could afterward.

Alex looked dazed at the brief church service, and politely thanked everyone for coming. She and Alice were the only women there. There had never been another woman in Paul's life after his wife. He had remained faithful to her memory. For all his worldly modern interests and points of view, he had lived by his traditional, old-fashioned values and principles. Work had been his religion, and family. He wasn't interested in worldly possessions or amassing a great fortune. He had a nice house and property and some family heirlooms, but he was never interested in showing off, and had put most of what he earned back into the business. He died shortly before his seventy-first birthday, and would probably have lived a great deal longer, were it not for the Spanish flu, which had cut so many lives short, in addition to the staggering losses in the war.

Alex left a message at her advisor's office at the university, to inform them that her grandfather had died, and that she would not return before the Christmas break and would make up for the work in January. She had family business to attend to.

That proved to be truer than she realized. Paul's attorney, John Kelly, gave her three days' grace when he saw how devastated she looked at the funeral. He hadn't understood how attached she was to Paul, or how much grief she'd suffered. He came to see her four days after her grandfather died, and she looked shaken and pale. She seemed traumatized, but was respectful and serious and paid attention to what he said. Everything he told her came as a surprise. Paul had made some very clearly defined decisions on his deathbed, and had signed all the necessary documents to enforce it. Everything was in order. Paul wasn't a man who left important things to chance, or open to interpretation. He had been crystal clear with his attorney and entirely lucid when he altered his will.

He had left everything to Alex—his house and its contents, his newspaper, and his money. He didn't have an enormous fortune, but he had a very respectable amount of money, which would serve her well for a very long time. She wasn't an heiress to a great inheritance, but she was a woman of means now. Added to what her father and grandmother had left her, and the apartment she still owned in France, she had a considerable amount of money to keep her safe and protect her. And even more, if she sold the paper one day, or Paul's home and property.

He had intended for the newspaper to be sold when he died, and to leave her the proceeds of the sale. But having met her and knowing her well now, and given what he believed her capable of eventually, with education and experience, he thought she could run the paper one day. Not for a long time, and she needed to learn from the very experienced people he had left in place to run it, with bequests to them as well, in acknowledgment of the valuable services they provided. But he felt sure that in a decade or so, Alex would be able to run the paper if she chose to, or sell it wisely if she preferred. He left it up to her, and he hoped it would give her as much pleasure and satisfaction as it had given him. He thought her a very capable young woman, who with time and age could run *The Beardstown Courier* as well as any man, or as well as he had himself. The attorney pointed out to her that it was a great tribute to her.

"Your grandfather had great faith in you. He wanted Josiah to continue running it for as long as possible, and for you to learn from him. He didn't expect you to work at the paper now. He wanted you to continue your education, travel, maybe work at another newspaper to gain experience. He thought you might want to live in New York for a few years after college. He didn't expect you to get tied down here for quite some time. In fact he hoped you wouldn't. The paper is in good hands now with the people who work for him. He didn't want you to shoulder it just yet. He wanted you to have a broader life experience first," he explained. Alex nodded, feeling dazed. It was hard to fully understand all that she owned now, and the possibilities she had for the future. Her grandfather had left her room to make her own decisions. Nothing he had given her was conditional. If she wanted to, she could sell everything at any time, and never see Beardstown again. It was not only a generous legacy, but he had thought it all out carefully, and addressed it in detail in his will.

"I'm very grateful," Alex said in a choked voice. She was also stunned and confused. She owned a newspaper now, which she didn't have to run, but could one day, and she owned a home, if she wanted to live there, now or later. He had protected and provided for her in every possible way. She couldn't have wished for more, except that she would have preferred to have him alive, and own none of it herself, and have him enjoying the fruit of his labors for many years. She had wanted nothing from him, except his love.

"Nothing will change for now," John Kelly added. "He very strongly wanted you to continue your education." At her age, she could very easily have decided to go crazy, indulge herself, and spend it all, and the lawyer had been afraid of that, as someone so young, but her grandfather knew her better. The attorney could see now that she was a solid young woman, with a good head on her shoulders, and Paul had said proudly, with a smile, that Alex had a mind of her own. Her mind was racing, considering what she should do now.

"Can I still work at the paper in the summer?" she asked in an awestruck voice.

"You can do whatever you like, Miss Bouvier," the lawyer said respectfully. "You own *The Beardstown Courier*. You can work there whenever you want. He just didn't want you to try running it too soon, until you're ready. He said you're a very talented writer," John Kelly said admiringly. He had grown up in Beardstown too. He had studied in Chicago, gone to law school at Princeton, and come back to his hometown. It wasn't just a town of backward farmers—there were educated people there.

"I'd like to work at the paper in the summer like I did last year," she said softly. She seemed very meek to John, but she was shaken to her core by what she had just inherited. It was a lot to deal with for a girl of eighteen, but her grandfather had left it to her in the best possible way. He had great faith in her, and trusted her completely, more than she felt she deserved. And he was so clear in his thinking that he had been able to set it up quickly and efficiently before he died, according to his wishes. The minute he realized how sick he was and what could happen, he called Kelly.

The attorney left her to think about it, after he had explained it all to her, and gave her a copy of the will that she could examine on her own.

Alex wasn't able to do any studying during the Christmas break—she was too distracted by everything that had happened, and by trying to figure out her future. She wasn't as sure as her grandfather that she would be capable of running the paper one day, but she did want to learn in detail, from the people running it now, what she'd need to know to take it over one day. It would be a mammoth task, and she didn't know how a man would feel, if she married, about having a wife who owned a newspaper and ran it. A husband might make her sell it, and she didn't want to, and hoped she would never have to.

She didn't celebrate Christmas at all. Her heart wasn't in it. Before the holiday, she had a meeting with Josiah Webster and the associate editor, Walter Strong, to assure them that she didn't intend to make any changes now, nor to work there for a long, long time. They were grateful for the reassurance, and that she didn't want to sell the paper. They loved it, not quite as much as Paul had, but nearly.

Josiah couldn't imagine a woman running it, and thought it would be too much for her. He was the same age as Paul but not as modern in his thinking. Paul thought she could do a good job of it one day, as long as she didn't try to take it over too quickly. He had made that clear in his will.

"I'd like to work at the paper next summer," she said simply. "Like last year, as an intern." Josiah smiled at the thought that their new owner was a teenager who would be their errand girl, but it was all she wanted for now. And to continue to write the column she had started, the way her grandfather had suggested, on women's issues. Paul had wanted more fresh blood in their management, and Alex was certainly that. She was barely out of the schoolroom. Josiah hoped she wouldn't rush it, but she didn't seem inclined to. The men left the meeting with a lot to think about, and so did Alex.

She finished her papers for school three days before she went back to Chicago. It had been a brutally sad, lonely holiday for her without her grandfather. She had come to love him so much, and they had made such wonderful plans that would never happen now. She was grateful for the months she had had with him, and felt his absence acutely.

She looked thinner and very serious when she went back to Chicago. She said that her grandfather had died, to explain her absence, but she said nothing about the inheritance to anyone.

The contents of the will were confidential, and no one at the newspaper knew about them either, only the two men who ran it, and would continue to do so. There were no visible changes, except in ownership, and future changes would depend on what Alex did and decided.

She turned in her papers at the university, and was given a makeup exam for the test she had missed. Everything was being disrupted due to the Spanish flu—schools, offices, businesses, colleges, everyone's social lives and plans. And families, as the main breadwinners died and women were faced with figuring out how to support their families, or men were faced with bringing up children as widowers. Between the impact of the pandemic, and broken men returning from the war, traumatized by their experiences and most without jobs, it was a sober time for the country. In contrast, the economy had been boosted by the war.

Men were combing the country for jobs, and some women were as well. They had been forced to function without the help of men for four years of war in Europe, and a year and a half in the States. So many of the men were so damaged from what they had seen and done, and what had been done to them, in battle, the male population was greatly reduced and seemed danger-ously unstable, and millions of people were dying from the Span-ish flu, which impacted the economy. Many businesses were closed, or understaffed, and failing.

Alex struggled every day with her grief over losing her grandfa-ther, and in February, two months after his death, she had an unexpected opportunity. The professor of a literature class she was taking said that a friend of his who worked for a major newspaper was looking for summer interns to work at the paper, and he had thought of her since she had frequently expressed her interest in journalism.

She was surprised when he asked her. "In Chicago?" she inquired, and he shook his head. That was the hitch.

"In New York." It was at *The New York World,* a very popular newspaper with a strong voice. Her grandfather had read it often, just to keep abreast of the competition. It had a circulation of a million readers.

"I don't know anyone in New York," she said, about to thank him and say no.

"You can always stay at a women's hotel, you'd be safe there." He knew it wouldn't be inexpensive, but there were many such hotels, so women could travel and visit the city safely, as she had when she arrived from Europe alone, and had spent a night in New York. They were safer than ordinary hotels, with no men staying there. "It's not a paid position—internships usually aren't—but it would be great experience, if you're serious about working for a newspaper one day." He had no idea that she already owned one. But it sounded like the kind of job her grandfather had wanted her to have, to broaden her exposure. And she'd loved New York when she was there.

"It sounds interesting. Can I think about it? I already have a summer internship lined up, but this sounds better and more exciting."

"It's a great paper," he said, which she knew. "I can wait a few days to tell him," he said easily, and she thanked him for considering her and suggesting it.

She wrestled with the idea for two days, and finally couldn't resist it. It could be a lot of fun, and hard work, and she had a feeling her grandfather would think it a good idea and would want her to go. She could have a summer internship at her own paper any time, but a chance to have one at a New York paper with such a high circulation might not come again.

She thanked her professor for the opportunity, and told him she would be open to it, and he replied that he would give her name to his friend and a strong recommendation.

A week later, *The New York World* offered her the summer internship and she accepted. She booked a room for two months at the Martha Washington, where she had stayed before. It was even conveniently located for her job, which was from the first of July to the first of September. It even gave her a month at home in June before she had to report for work.

Josiah Webster said they would be sorry not to see her at the *Courier* that summer, but hoped she would enjoy a brief stint in New York. He didn't say that he wouldn't have wanted his own daughter alone in New York for a summer, but Alex was an independent young woman, and her circumstances were different— she had no family supervision now.

Alex was excited at the prospect of her summer internship. They had two openings, the one they had given her and another for a male student, and had chosen a young man from Harvard. Their accepting her for the summer job was a distinct honor for her.

She could hardly wait for July, and it gave her something to look forward to, as she recovered slowly from the loss of her grandfather, and completed her first year at the University of Chicago with excellent grades. She missed being able to share her thoughts and observations with her grandfather, and she had valued his advice. She was going to have to figure things out for herself now. The summer internship in New York was the first step into the future that lay ahead of her.

Alex was startled in May when a fellow student, a boy from her English Lit class, congratulated her on the internship in New York. She hadn't made many close friends that year, except Yoko, her roommate in the dorm, and she had left school in March, when her father died of the Spanish flu in San Francisco. She had gone home to console her mother, and it wasn't clear whether or not she was coming back. Alex had been alone in her dorm room ever since. She had no friends so far among the male students. She was too shy to talk to them and everyone's fears about the flu made dating complicated and unappealing.

The boy who spoke to her about the internship was tall and athletic-looking, blond and handsome. He had heard about her summer job from the instructor who had suggested her for it. The boy's name was Albert Smith. All she knew about him was that his father was a famous architect, which he had mentioned once in class. She had noticed that he seemed to have a lot of friends and was gregarious. He had glanced at her before, but had never spoken to her. She was surprised when he stopped to talk to her as they left class. It was sunny and warm and spring had finally reached Chicago.

"You're going to have a great time in New York this summer," he said enviously. "I would have loved it, but your grades are better than mine."

"Not always," she said modestly. "And Mr. Kravits knows I want to be a writer and study journalism."

"I want to be an architect like my dad," he admitted.

"That's why he didn't suggest you for it," she said pleasantly, as they walked down the hall together. She had a break in classes until that afternoon. Albert was the first boy who had taken an interest in her and approached her. She was unaware of her looks, and surprised when boys spoke to her. With their blond hair, she and Albert looked somewhat alike, except he was much taller.

"Are you from Chicago?" he asked her. They had been in the same lit class for four months without speaking before.

"Beardstown," she said, and he smiled.

"Did you grow up on a farm?" He looked a little supercilious as he said it.

"No. I grew up in Paris. I came here a year ago to live with my grandfather. He ran a newspaper, hence the internship," she said succinctly. He had noticed both her slight accent and the past tense.

"He doesn't run the paper anymore? Did he retire?" He was curious about her now—she looked pretty and animated when they talked. She was normally quiet and kept to herself after class.

"He died in December, of the flu," she said simply, and he looked awkward.

"I'm sorry. Would you like to have lunch?" It was a peace offering to make up for his faux pas. She had plenty of time before her next class and she accepted.

They went to a sandwich shop near the university, which she'd been to before. They both ordered sandwiches and lemonade and sat down. He was very good-looking and seemed nice.

By the end of lunch, she knew he had two sisters and a brother, he was the youngest, and they had a house on the lake. They spent summers in Maine and he liked to play tennis and sail. She could tell from the way he was dressed, and from talking to him, that his family had money. He said they had been to Europe several times before the war. He was twenty and both his sisters were married. His brother was in law school at Columbia. His pedigree was clearly above reproach. She didn't find him exciting, just handsome, and he was having trouble figuring her out. She lived in a hick town in an agricultural community, but had grown up in Paris. Her grandfather ran a newspaper. She didn't talk about her debut or give any of the clear signals that would have suggested a fancy aristocratic background, and yet she seemed very dignified and sophisticated, and very bright. And she had gotten a prize internship in New York. He wondered if she was the daughter or granddaughter of anyone important. He didn't think so, but he wasn't sure. Alex could sense where he was going with his questions. He asked if she was going back to Paris now that the war was over. He assumed she had come to the States to escape the war.

"I don't think so," she said.

"What does your father do in Paris?" he asked more bluntly.

"He was a doctor, and my mother was a nurse. She worked for him. They died in the war. My mother grew up in Beardstown—that's why I came here to live with her father."

"I'm sorry, that's awful about your parents. I got drafted but I had scarlet fever when I was five, and I have a heart murmur. It doesn't bother me, but it kept me out of the war. I'm glad. I didn't want to go to war. My brother got drafted too, but my father talked to some people he knew, and he got sent to Washington to work for a congressman. He loved it, and after that he went to law school when the war ended." It was obvious that he was well connected, very smooth, and seemed to have led a charmed life compared to her experience during the war.

"My parents worked at a field hospital at the front lines." She really didn't want to talk about the war, but she had nothing else in common with him. More than anything, he seemed spoiled and boring. He was intrigued by her, and the little he knew about her. Most of all, he was taken with her looks, but her life story sounded intriguing, and unfortunate, given the parents and grandfather she'd lost to the flu and the war.

They had run out of things to say to each other by the end of lunch. She wished him a good summer, and he wished her a good time in New York.

She thought about him afterward. There had been no important boy in her life since Julien three years before. She was only nineteen now, and she knew that other girls her age were desperate to get married, and some already were, in the rural communities like Beardstown, and some even had children by the time they were her age. She couldn't imagine it. There was so much she wanted to do, and to learn, about writing and newspapers and life.

With so many men lost in the war, the competition to meet boys like Albert would be fierce. He was healthy, whole, handsome, and undamaged, he hadn't lost his sight to nerve gas, nor would he be screaming in the night from nightmares about what he'd seen in the trenches and on the battlefields. He hadn't been wounded, or killed anyone. But Alex couldn't see herself with someone like him. She'd rather be alone, and with everything her grandfather had left her, she didn't have to marry, if she didn't want to. He had given her freedom, protection, and independence for as long as she wanted it. Maybe forever. Forever sounded perfect to her for now. She had never been in love, despite kissing Julien at sixteen and Phillip Baxter at eighteen on the ship. They were boys. For the moment, there was so much she wanted to do, and she didn't want a man who would interfere or disapprove or tell her what to do. She was free, and she liked it that way. Her grandfather had given her the greatest gift, the freedom to live the life she wanted, whenever she figured out what that was.

Chapter 8

Alex got a month to relax in Beardstown at the end of her freshman year at the University of Chicago. She planned to take the walks on her grandfather's property that she had taken with him the year before. The weather was warm and balmy, and she wanted to visit the offices of the *Courier* and see the people she knew and had worked with the previous summer. Word had leaked out that she owned the paper now, which was remarkable for a girl of nineteen, but she had no involvement on a daily working basis, and Josiah Webster was still running the *Courier* with the same iron hand. If anything, he was tougher now that Paul Peterson was no longer alive. Paul had had a warmer, more humane, collegial style than Josiah, and was always open to new ideas. Josiah was more traditional than Paul had been and was more determined than ever to keep the *Courier* appealing, successful, and profitable, and he was less of a risk-taker than Paul. Alex missed her grandfather's editorial columns, as did all of their readers. He had his own personal style. She still wanted to work on her editorial columns once a month, as her grandfather had hoped, but hadn't found her distinctive voice yet. She wanted to have a unique signature style like her grandfather one day.

When she got home to Beardstown from Chicago at the end of May, the ongoing page-one top story was still the Spanish flu. The number of deaths had dropped slightly for no reason anyone could determine. The winter before, as the troops returned from abroad, they brought the virus with them from Europe, and innocently infected Americans they came in contact with in every walk of life as they rejoined their families and friends, returned to their businesses and jobs, and infected the workplace and every aspect of American life. Other countries were experiencing the same thing. It was beginning to abate now, seven months later. After Paul Peterson died of the Spanish flu, the paper printed a black border around the front page for a month, in honor of him.

The second day of Alex's month-long stay there in June was a landmark day for American women. After being defeated twice in the last year, the Nineteenth Amendment passed the Senate, giving women the right to vote, on June fourth, 1919. It had been hard-earned and hard-won, and bravely fought for, for nearly ten years, by passionate women who had been willing to risk life and limb and had sacrificed their lives in some cases to give American women the right to vote.

Alex was delighted and the *Courier* ran a banner headline the next day, as did most newspapers in the nation.

Other than that historical event, it was a quiet month, with the ongoing devastating statistics of the Spanish flu. Some people compared it to the Black Plague of the fifteenth century. It was continuing to ravage its way around the globe, affecting all socioeconomic levels, all races, and all ages, with the elderly hardest hit, like Alex's grandfather and grandmother. People had gotten more careful in the past year. Schools and some offices were closed, theaters were closed, masks were mandatory, and cemeteries were overwhelmed. It was hard to believe, as Alex looked out at the peaceful countryside surrounding her grandfather's home. Farms were affected too. She knew she'd have to be even more careful in New York.

Alex took the Broadway Limited from Union Station in Chicago on Friday the twenty-seventh of June, having spent a day shopping at Marshall Field's in Chicago before she left, to make sure she had the appropriate clothes to wear in the office, with gloves and hats. She didn't want to draw attention to herself with anything too fashionable, but she had to look ladylike and proper. She enjoyed the observation car on the train and arrived in New York at Penn Station the morning of Saturday, June 28th, and checked into the Martha Washington Hotel again, with a bigger room this time since she would be there for two months.

The first of July was a Tuesday, and Alex arrived at the newspaper precisely on time in a gray linen suit with midcalf hemline, a matching hat, and white gloves. She was wearing a thin white silk blouse under her jacket. She looked beautiful and older than her nineteen years in the elegant suit, which she'd bought in Chicago. It wasn't showy, and it fit her slim figure perfectly.

She reported to the woman she'd been assigned to in personnel, Monica Gonzales. She was older, with dark hair pulled back in a tight bun, and she was wearing a black summer suit. It was a warm day.

"You've been assigned to our society pages," she told Alex with a businesslike demeanor. It felt like a dream to Alex just being there. The building was huge, with newspaper delivery trucks parked outside that would travel the city all night with the last edition. Her assignment sounded like fun. The woman gave her a slip of paper with the floor and office number on it and the name of her supervisor, the head of Society, Sylvia Bates. Monica sent Alex on her way within minutes, and she put on her mask and went back to the elevators. The Society offices were on the eleventh floor, and five minutes later, she reached them. There was a front room bustling with activity, with six young women crowded together at desks, typing furiously on large typewriters. There were three offices behind them, with windows, for the editors who worked on those pages. One was in charge of weddings, the second one parties, and the third was for "encounters"—celebrities and socialites seen at various events. And there was a long wall with an enormous bulletin board with photographs pinned to it. Everyone looked busy, and all the women at desks were wearing masks because of the flu. Alex was wearing hers when she arrived. The women in the front room glanced at Alex with interest. The one nearest her took her mask off and smiled. She looked stressed, and it was only nine-twenty in the morning.

"Can I help you?" She thought Alex was dropping off news of an engagement or impending wedding.

"I'm the summer intern," Alex said, trying not to sound as terrified as she was. She had no experience at all with a "society column," and had never seen one. The *Courier* didn't have one, and Beardstown didn't need one.

"I'm Melanie Pratt," the young woman said in a friendly tone. She pointed to an empty desk behind them with a typewriter on it. "Grab a desk, take off your hat, and wait for someone to ask you for something. You can ask me if you need directions. What's your name?"

"Alexandra Bouvier. Alex."

"I thought you were a bride." Melanie laughed at her mistake and put her mask back on, as Alex made her way to the back desk, put her purse underneath, her jacket on the back of the chair, and her hat on the desk. She was ready for action.

Ten minutes later, a tall, elegant woman with a blond chignon, around fifty, exploded out of her office and addressed the front room. "The Patterson/Argyle wedding was just canceled. Pull all the pictures we've got. And we need to change the layout, pronto. We were saving space for the reception. We've got to kill it." Everyone began scurrying, and Melanie whispered to Alex that the tall blonde was Sylvia Bates, the chief editor of the department. "Try to stay out of her way," Melanie whispered, and five minutes later, the woman emerged from her office again and pointed at Alex. "You! Go downstairs and get me the layout I sent down yesterday. We have to figure out what to run instead. I hate to use it, but I think the Larocca/Genovese wedding might work. The Laroccas are spending a million on it. It will be vulgar but spectacular." Alex nodded, feeling dazed, and as soon as Sylvia went back to her office, Alex rushed to Melanie's desk, and spoke in a whisper.

"Where do I go, and who do I see?" Melanie scribbled instructions on a piece of paper and handed it to Alex.

"It's in the basement—ask for Joey, and tell him to give you all the photographs for the wedding they just canceled. And don't panic. You'll be fine. You'll get used to it here." Alex nodded, speechless with fear, clung to the piece of paper, and hurried out of the room. She found the basement filing room easily, and Joey turned out to be a big bear of a man who gave her an armload of photographs of the bride to return to Miss Bates. She thanked Joey, rushed back to the elevator, and completed her mission.

For the next three hours she handed out typing paper and carbons, carried photographs from one office to another, delivered mail, poured coffee, sharpened and distributed pencils, tried to stay out of everyone's way and keep their requests and instructions straight, and answered the phone in between. She was an errand girl for the department, and the tasks she accomplished were a blur when she tried to remember them, and she didn't know anyone's name yet except Sylvia Bates, and Melanie, who was a godsend, and translated all the mission directions for Alex. By noon, her head was pounding and her hands were shaking she was so nervous. Melanie stopped at her desk for a minute.

"You can go to lunch now," she told her, and Alex had no idea where to go. "Straight down the street left of here, there's a good deli, or there's the cafeteria downstairs in the basement. The food stinks, but it's faster. There's always a line at the deli, so it's slow, but the sandwiches are great. Be back in forty-five minutes." It was exactly twelve-thirty. "Bates goes to lunch at one, and she'll be out for two hours," she whispered, and Alex nodded, hurried to her desk, grabbed her jacket and ran to the elevator. She had decided that the basement was safer. She didn't want to come back late, even if the boss was out, in case someone squealed on her. No one had spoken to her so far except Melanie, and Sylvia Bates, who didn't know or care who she was. She had feet to run and hands to carry things, which was all Sylvia Bates wanted from her. Whether or not she had a brain was immaterial, for now, but might matter later.

Alex grinned as she went downstairs in the freight elevator, with newspapers stacked high in it. It was exciting being there, and if she hadn't been so nervous, she would have enjoyed it, but it was fun anyway. The furor of activity in the enormous building and number of employees made the *Courier* look like an amateur operation in comparison. But she knew that this was the kind of experience she needed, a big city operation, to teach her the skills she'd require one day to apply to the *Courier*.

She reached the basement quickly and found the cafeteria. She had a chicken sandwich and a yogurt, and iced tea, ate quickly, and then wandered out into the hall in the basement. She saw a huge room of men across the hall, each with a desk, some with phones, some with hats on. The room was noisy—there were the sounds of phones ringing, men calling to each other, and laughter. It was the antithesis of the office of women she was working in upstairs, which was neat, small, and quiet.

A young man hurried out of the big room as she walked by and crashed into her, almost knocking her over, and he grabbed her arms to steady her with an apologetic look. He looked to be in his late twenties or thirty, and he looked her over with an appreciative glance and held onto her arms for a minute, which made her blush. She had dropped her jacket, and he picked it up from the floor and handed it to her.

"Whoa . . . we have a princess in our midst. I'm sorry I tried to knock you down. I'm Sam, who are you, and where did you come from? What took you so long to get here?" She laughed at his brash approach. He was good-looking. He had his jacket off and his shirt sleeves rolled up, and had taken off his tie in the heat.

"I'm Alex. From upstairs. The society pages."

"I should have known." He grinned at her. "I hope you're not a bride." She shook her head and laughed at him. "We're Crime," he said happily, gesturing to the room full of men behind him. They were all reporters and photographers and there was a cloud of smoke hanging above them, like the bowels of hell, but they all seemed to be having a good time and were talking a lot and laughing. "Do you play cards, Princess?" he asked her, and she nodded. "If you get bored with the brides, come down here, you can play cards with us. We're here twenty-four hours a day. People commit murder at all hours." A second man approached them then. He looked older, in his forties, was balding, had a cigar in his hand, and looked at Sam with disgust, with an apologetic glance at Alex, who was enjoying the exchange.

"Are you at it again? Leave the poor girl alone." He turned to Alex then. "I'm sorry, he's incorrigible. We normally keep him chained up, but he gets loose occasionally."

"She's from Society," Sam informed his coworker, who said his name was Tommy. He had the same rough-around-the-edges style as Sam, but they were both fun to talk to, and couldn't keep their eyes off her.

"You can tell. They hide us in the basement," Tommy said. "We're not couth enough to be upstairs, and there are too many of us. Murder is our number-one big seller. I'm sure there are more homicides in New York than weddings. Other than that, the world specializes in sports, sex, and scandal."

"Murder is more fun. Crime is a big feature for us. The guys in Finance are all half dead, and they're all weird in Travel. Arts and Leisure are really weird. And the book reviewers are too serious. I never know what they're talking about. Stick with us," Sam said. "Drop by anytime."

Alex glanced at her watch then, and panicked. "I have to go."

"See ya 'round, Princess," Sam said with a wave, as she rushed toward the elevator, and the two reporters from Crime walked into the cafeteria for another pot of coffee. "She's a knockout," Sam commented admiringly as they waited for the coffee.

"And you'll be our next crime scene if you start hitting on the girls from Society. They're all debutantes and some rich guy's daughter. They work here for free as summer interns. The women we know can't afford to do that. You mess with the girls from Society, and their fathers will kill you. Trust me. And by next year, they will all be married, and not to guys like us."

"She's gorgeous," Sam said with a grin, and Tommy pointed an imaginary gun at him.

"Bang, you're dead. Stay away from the debutantes!" he said as they collected their coffeepot and went back to the smoke-filled room of reporters.

Alex was back in the Society office by then, and Melanie asked her where she ate.

"The cafeteria. I didn't want to be late getting back."

"I forgot to warn you about the Crime boys. They're right across the hall, and they're all nuts, and go after anything in a skirt." Alex smiled at the description.

"I met two of them."

"They're all the same. They're the randiest guys in the building. They act like they haven't seen a woman in years. Some of them are fun. They report on the worst crime scenes in the city. I think it makes them a little nuts." Alex had experienced it first-hand, and didn't mind. Melanie showed her where everything was then, since they had a little time before the three editors came back from lunch.

When they did, the big news that afternoon was a major film star who had been caught at a hotel for a weekend tryst with a famous socialite, who happened to be married, and his wife was filing for divorce. It was the hot story of the hour. And the canceled Patterson/Argyle wedding instantly became old news, sank beneath the waters of the society column, and vanished. The heartbroken bride was no longer of interest. Alex heard later that the groom had dumped the bride to go back to his ex-girlfriend, whose father was offering him a million dollars to marry her, and he needed the money. There were no secrets in the offices of the society column, and all the juiciest social news in the city was grist for their mill.

All the women in the Society office left at five. The girls at the front of the office were single, and of the three editors, two were divorced, and one had never married—Sylvia, Melanie said, was the mistress of a very wealthy married man, and she kept him by knowing all of his secrets.

Alex's head was spinning as she walked back to her hotel. She had been running all day. None of it was serious journalism, but it was fascinating. The society column was the spice that women loved in the newspaper. Sports and finance kept the men happy, and Alex wondered if anyone really cared about the news. It was very different from her grandfather's thorough, deep, and at times philosophical reports of world news. His was a high-quality brand of journalism, whereas this was fare for everyone, whatever their tastes or interests. She smiled, remembering her exchange with the two Crime reporters. But doubtless theirs was grim work, and they needed a little levity to balance it.

She fell asleep at nine o'clock that night. And the next day was more of the same. She ate at the cafeteria again, and ran into

Sam. He invited her into the room to meet some of his coworkers, and before she could stop him, he had guided her into the
room full of male reporters. They looked at her like hungry lions
having a piece of meat waved at them, and she escaped as soon
as she could. When she got back to her office, Melanie made a
face.

"Whew! I know where you've been. You reek of cheap cigars.
Did the Crime guys hassle you again?"

"They kidnapped me for a few minutes, and I ran."

"I can smell it. Someone needs to take a hose to them. It's
weird, either the guys down there are jokesters, or they're depressed and don't talk at all. They see some really ugly stuff, the
worst side of the human race. And the Mafia families don't help.
They do some incredibly bad things, and the guys in Crime see
all of it."

"They're supposedly worse in Chicago," Alex said knowledg-
ably, but she knew her grandfather had refused to cover Mafia
news. He said they were the worst element of the business, and
he hated organized crime.

She tried the deli for lunch on Thursday with Melanie, and
she was right, the food was better, although the service was slow.
But she didn't see the Crime reporters as a result. The Society
staff got notified of three more engagements that day, and they
had four big weddings to cover that weekend. They used outside
photographers to cover them, who were of a much higher caliber
than the ones who worked on staff, and were kept busy with
homicides.

Friday was the Fourth of July holiday, so they had a three-day weekend. Alex finished the week on Thursday with a flourish, having completed every task she'd been assigned. She was efficient, hardworking, and fast, and all three editors had noticed her. Even Sylvia Bates was impressed and thanked her, which Melanie said was high praise.

Melanie and Alex wished each other a good weekend. They had their weekends free. The editors attended the weddings they covered to make sure everything went smoothly, that the coverage remained respectful and in good taste, and that no one from the paper offended anyone at the wedding. And Sylvia knew who all the players were. She had been running the society column for the *World* for twenty-five years and no one did it better.

By the end of the week, Alex admired her. Sylvia Bates was a consummate professional, and the wedding coverage was exquisite, better than *Vogue*.

In her hotel room that night, Alex wished that she could tell her grandfather about it. She thought he'd be amused.

Alex spent the Fourth of July weekend visiting museums she hadn't seen the year before on her one day in New York, and she walked along the East River and took a carriage ride around the city on her own and loved it.

She was excited all over again on Monday when she got to work, at the same time Sylvia Bates arrived at the office.

"How were the weddings?" Alex asked her politely, in awe of the elegant woman who was her boss. She was the essence of chic and good taste. What she wore didn't cost a fortune, but she knew just how to put it together for maximum effect. She was impeccable in a crisp white linen dress, without a hair out of place.

"Two of them were exquisite and perfectly done, on their Long Island estates." She had covered two in one day. "The Larocca was alarmingly garish, and you have to wonder how many bodies are buried under their front lawn and in their flower beds." The Laroccas were one of the biggest crime families in New York, but had achieved near respectability by marrying debutantes with money-hungry fathers. It had put them on the society pages nonetheless, which in a cynical way amused Sylvia, so on occasion she indulged them. "Everything about it was wrong, but so much so that it actually became right, if you know what I mean. They spent a hundred thousand dollars on the dress. But the food was fabulous, and they flew the band in from somewhere. Every crooked politician in the state was there, so no one wore masks." There were fines now for not wearing them in public, and a ban on large gatherings, but compared to mass murder, it was a minor offense. "Is that an accent I detect?" she asked Alex with a piercing look. She noticed every detail, and was a keen observer.

"I'm French," Alex confessed. "But my mother was American."

"How long have you been here?" Sylvia asked more gently. She could be kind when she wanted to be, and she sensed a story there.

"A little over a year."

"In New York?"

"In a little farm town two hundred miles outside Chicago. But I attend the University of Chicago. My mother went there too."

"It's a good school." Sylvia smiled at Alex then. She had no children of her own, and had never wanted any. She had poured herself into her career heart and soul. "Good girl. You're smart to get an education. It's the only way to make something of yourself." She had gone to Barnard. "Is this just a summer lark for you, or are you serious about it?"

"Very serious," Alex responded. And Sylvia could see it was true.

"Good. Then make sure you learn something here, and make it count."

"I intend to. I'm very grateful to be here," she said, and Sylvia nodded, marched into her office, and closed the door.

It was a busy Monday morning in the Society department. The boys from Crime didn't accost Alex when she went to the cafeteria, got her lunch, and sat down alone at a table. She had gotten a list of the weddings they were covering for the next month, and was reading it carefully when a man walked up to her table and startled her.

"Mind if I sit down here? There are no free seats anywhere else." She glanced around and saw it was true, and nodded.

"Sure. Of course." She took her purse off the other chair, put it on the floor next to her, and went on reading, while he went to get his food. She paid no attention to him when he came back with a tray full of his lunch. She looked up at him. He was stern-looking and serious, with dark eyes and very dark hair. He was wearing a suit and tie, and he stared at her for a minute, and spoke before she could start reading again. He was handsome and looked to be in his mid- to late thirties. He didn't seem friendly and was very intense. She could almost feel the electricity flowing from him as he sat down across from her.

"You're the girl from Society all my colleagues are talking about, aren't you?" He said it like an accusation and she was sorry she'd agreed to let him sit with her. He looked respectable, but not friendly.

"I hope not. What are they saying?"

"What you'd expect. That you're beautiful, what they say about the deb of the hour every year."

"I'm not a deb," she said coolly, on the verge of deciding she didn't like him, and he was a jerk. "I'm a summer intern," she said with dignity.

"Same thing. You're not getting paid, so it's safe to assume your father is supporting you, unless you're married. But if you were, you wouldn't be working here."

She didn't like his assumptions about her. "You're correct, I'm not married. But my father is not supporting me. I'm supporting myself," on her inheritance from her grandfather, so he wasn't entirely wrong. He appeared to have a chip on his shoulder the size of a mountain.

"Sorry," he said, softening a little, and she hated to admit he was movie-star handsome, but his scowl didn't improve his looks. "We working stiffs are jealous of people with rich fathers."

"I don't have a rich father," she said simply, or any father, she didn't say. "You're in Crime?" It was her turn to guess, and he nodded, amused.

"How can you tell, by my charming personality, or my ill humor? Looking at dead bodies every day doesn't improve my mood or my faith in human nature."

"Then why don't you report on something else?" she said sensibly, sipping her lemonade, while he tried to ignore how beautiful she was. She had a perfect face and a kind expression. "Like finance, or sports," she suggested.

"Sports bore me, and I'm terrible at math. Actually, finance bores me too. And I'm good at what I do. Do you like working on all those weddings? At least the affairs they ferret out are amusing."

"You're not married?"

He shook his head. "Are you?"

She laughed in answer. "No. I'm only nineteen."

"Lots of women are married by nineteen. Some girls consider it the only career open to them."

"Sometimes they're right. I want to work for a newspaper one day. And not just on weddings."

"It's the only job they'll give you here. There are no women in the other departments. Except art, maybe, but they're all weird. Maybe the women in your department think the weddings will be contagious," he said, and she laughed again. He had an edge to him but he had a sense of humor.

"If they are contagious, I'll quit immediately," she said with a wry smile.

"You don't want to get married?" He was surprised, if it was true.

"No, I don't. Not for a long time if I do, or maybe ever."

"Why not?" He was intrigued by her. He hadn't sat down with her in order to meet her—his reason had been real—but now he was enjoying her. She was smart and funny and a good sparring partner. His colleagues hadn't said that about her. Just that she was beautiful, which was also true. But there was more to her.

"It's too complicated to explain," she said vaguely. She had decided after the losses of the last few years that she didn't want to lose any more people, or love anyone enough to care. She had lost her entire family, which seemed like more than enough. She had no family left now, and wanted to keep it that way. Love was a game that seemed too risky, and the stakes were too high, but she didn't say it to him. He could sense there was a story there, and not a happy one. "What about you?" she asked him. "Do you want to get married?"

"Never. Are you planning to propose? If you are, I strongly advise against it," he said, and she laughed. She had a wonderful free laugh like a child and he loved the sound. It made him smile. He was better looking when he did. "Well, now that we've established that neither of us wants to get married, I think it would be safe to have lunch again. I'd like that. Would you?" he asked her directly, and she nodded. "I'm too old for you anyway, so you're safe. I'm thirty-six, seventeen years older than you. I could be your father."

"No, you couldn't," she said firmly.

"Why not?"

"You're much too grumpy and ill-natured to have children," she said innocently, and he laughed out loud.

"Touché. You are absolutely right." She glanced at her watch then.

"I have to get back to work. It was nice to meet you," she said with a smile.

"I enjoyed it too. I'm Oliver Foster. Ollie, to the people who can tolerate me. Of whom there are very few."

"Alexandra Bouvier. Alex." They shook hands across the table.

"You're French?" He could hear it now, but only slightly. She nodded. "Your English is excellent."

"My mother was American. I came here a year ago." He sensed that there was a story there too, and didn't want to ask and upset her. He liked her, in spite of appearances to the contrary. He liked her a lot. She seemed gutsy to him, and hadn't been intimidated by him. Most people were, which he preferred. He liked keeping people at bay.

"Where shall we have lunch next time?" he asked her.

"Here is fine," she said. She wasn't looking for a fancy lunch.

"You have very modest tastes," he said as they stood up. "Wednesday? One o'clock? I'm off tomorrow. I work on weekends. People love to murder each other on Saturdays." She was curious what he had done in the war, but didn't want to ask. He seemed to accept killing as commonplace, and to be hardened to it.

They walked out of the cafeteria together, at the exact moment that Tommy walked out of the room across the hall where they worked, and he was surprised to see them together.

"I see you two know each other, or did you just meet?" he commented, and neither of them answered. It was a fishing expedition and none of his business.

"See you," Alex said casually to Oliver. "Have a nice day off." She hurried to the elevator to go back upstairs. She was ten minutes late.

"Robbing the cradle, I see," Tommy teased Oliver.

"I'm thinking of adopting her," Oliver said easily, and walked past him with no further comment. Alex was smiling under the mask she had put back on in the crowded elevator. There was something very odd about Oliver Foster, in her opinion. Dark, unhappy, but incredibly smart, and she loved the way he laughed. All his cares seemed to slip away when he did. Getting a smile or a laugh out of him felt like a victory. And he was funny. She liked that about him too. She was looking forward to their lunch. As he sat down at his desk, thinking about her, so was he. For once, Sam and Tommy were right about her being a knockout. It was a first. She was ladylike and gutsy, and smart and interesting, and just shy enough to seem innocent and sweet. He was looking forward to lunch on Wednesday with Miss Alexandra Bouvier, *not* a debutante.

Chapter 9

On Tuesday, Alex did personal errands for Sylvia Bates. She bought silk stockings, and went to the dry cleaner for her. It was a menial job, but she enjoyed it anyway. She dropped off the dry cleaning at her home. Sylvia's apartment was beautiful, two floors in a private house on Fifth Avenue close to Washington Square. Sylvia had had the same exquisite taste in her decorating as she did in what she wore, and Alex enjoyed seeing it.

Alex worked with Pam MacDonald in the afternoon, who covered all the notable parties in the city. The Astors were giving a summer deb ball for their granddaughter at their Connecticut estate. Alex wondered what it would be like. Like Cinderella, she imagined. It would have been fun to go to an event like that once in her life, and wear a beautiful gown. She loved the fantasy of it, but wasn't sure if the reality would measure up to her girlish dreams. Her parents never went to important social events, all they did was work. Her grandfather had no social life at all. Her grandmother had gone to *thé dansants* in her youth, dances in the afternoon, which always sounded antiquated and sweet to Alex. The future she envisioned for herself was one of hard work too. Her dream was to write a book one day. In the meantime, she wrote short stories, and in her journal every night.

She wore a pale blue summer dress when she went to work on Wednesday. It was the color of her eyes, and she looked young and fresh when she met Oliver in the cafeteria for lunch. He left his office without telling anyone where he was going, and walked swiftly across the hall. They were the only department at the paper that didn't mind being across from the kitchen smells. At least it competed with their cigarettes and cigars. And it offered a constant supply of coffee and food, since they worked till all hours, and there was always someone on duty. The building was teeming with employees. Society was one of the smallest departments, and Crime one of the biggest. There were no female reporters in Crime. The subject was too rough.

"You look lovely," he commented as they went to get their food. It was a hot day, she was nervous meeting him, and she wasn't hungry, so she took a salad and some fruit with an iced tea. He took a hearty hot meal of pot roast and mashed potatoes, some vegetables, and a slice of pie. He ate his main meal at the paper, so he didn't have to cook or go out at night, and he was usually on the run from one crime scene to the next, watching some gang member get dragged off in handcuffs, or the police covering a body.

He paid for her lunch and they found a quiet corner table at the back of the room. The cafeteria wasn't busy yet, and the weather was so fine that most people wanted to leave the building, so there was no one around them, which was rare.

"Where did you grow up?" he asked her as they started lunch. She could see that he had a hearty appetite although it didn't show. He was fit and thin and athletic-looking.

"Paris, until last year," she said, picking at her salad. She'd never gotten used to big meals again, since the years of rationing in Paris, and she was still very slim.

"And where do you live now, when you're not a summer intern?" He was curious about her.

"I go to school in Chicago, at the University of Chicago, and my home is in Beardstown, Illinois, two hundred miles from there. It's beautiful farmland. I never thought I'd like to live on a farm, but it's nice, and very peaceful."

"More so than Paris in wartime, I suspect." She nodded. "Was Paris very tough during the war?" he asked her.

"Sometimes. There was no medicine, and rationing was really hard. We couldn't get milk, sugar, and eggs, or even meat sometimes, and anything fresh went to the army. My grandmother was a good cook so she made it work. I lived with her during the war. My parents were at the front."

"Both of them?" He looked surprised.

"My mother was a nurse."

"And your father?"

"He was a doctor." He didn't dare ask her where they were now. He sensed from the look in her eyes that he had ventured onto a minefield. She answered his silent question before he could ask. "They were killed in the war."

"They must have been very brave people," Oliver said respect-fully.

"They set up a field hospital at the front, it moved around to where the battles were. They saved a lot of lives. They were heroes," she said proudly.

"I'm sorry, Alex," he said sincerely. "I know what that's like. I lost my parents when I was young too. But not as gloriously as yours. My father drank himself to death before he was forty. And my mother was killed in an accident. She was skating with me and she fell through the ice. I couldn't save her. I wasn't strong enough to pull her up. I was twelve and help came too late." The horror of it was in Oliver's eyes, and heavy on her heart, for him.

"How awful." Alex could only imagine the impact on him. It wasn't surprising that there was a dark aura around him. She could see now that he had suffered a great deal.

"My father had already left her when it happened. I never saw him again after he left, and he didn't come to the funeral. I got shipped off to boarding school after my mother died. He died within the year. A group of distant relatives whom I never saw and didn't know paid for my schooling for the next six years, and then I came to New York, to go to Columbia School of Journal-ism on a scholarship, and here I am. We lived in Philadelphia until my mother died. And I spent six years in a boys' school just outside Boston after that."

"Were you in the army during the war?" she asked. They had gone straight to the hard subjects. He nodded.

"I was. I was lucky. They put me in military intelligence. I was thirty-four by the time we got into the war, and they figured I was too old to send to the front. I was stationed in London the entire time. Aside from the war, I loved it."

"My mother studied in England. She went to Oxford after Chicago, and the Sorbonne. I wanted to go to the Sorbonne, but I didn't apply because of the war. I didn't go to university until I came here. I really like Chicago." School was an easier subject than their lost parents. His seemed even more tragic than hers. Watching his mother die in front of him, being unable to save her, was an unimaginable horror, and having a drunken father who had abandoned them was a hard way to start life. It no longer surprised her that he seemed cynical, and had a difficult character. He had been punished early in life, and clearly had had no home life or contact with family to support him after his mother died. Alex had lost her parents but she'd had Mamie-Thérèse to love and comfort her. She was even more attentive and affectionate than her parents, who were so engrossed in their work. Mamie had all the time in the world for her. And she had a loving grandfather after that.

"It's brave of you to go to university," he said admiringly. "So many girls don't want to. They just want to get married and have babies. And even with an education, women are paid nothing. Your bosses in Society make a tenth what we do in Crime. It's disgusting." He looked outraged as he said it, and Alex was touched. "I marched with them last year, but it never makes a difference. They pay women dirt in every business. It's incredibly unfair."

"I know," Alex said. "At least we got the vote."

"Barely, and not in every state yet. Some states are still trying to block it. But they can't. The Senate passed it, and it's an amendment to the Constitution now. It's great that women got the vote, now they have to pay them a decent wage." He sounded like her parents and grandfather. And it shocked her to hear that the women who worked on the society column made a fraction of what he did.

"And women here make a lot more than women in France," she said with a fiery look in her eyes, and he smiled.

"And here I thought you were some spoiled debutante," he said with a smirk. "I never understand why those girls want internships. It's just a game to them. They're never going to work a day in their lives. They'll all be married in a year. And you're right to go to university, it's the only way you'll ever earn a decent wage. Education is essential, or women will be treated like slave labor forever."

"Most women can't afford an education," Alex said. Her grandfather had paid for hers, which she didn't tell Oliver.

As they talked, she found that they both burned for the same causes, which amounted to education, equality, and freedom for all. They covered a number of serious topics, unlike at their first meeting. She had more sympathy for him now, after hearing about his childhood. Maybe he had good reason to be bitter. It sounded like he came from a decent family, with some money, and had had terrible luck, which was true of Alex too.

She hadn't been totally honest with him. She told him that her grandfather had worked for a newspaper, but not that he owned it. And certainly not that now she did. She was afraid that Oliver would hate her for that, and think she was spoiled and rich.

"What newspaper does he write for?" Oliver asked her, not realizing that her grandfather had died.

"*The Beardstown Courier.* Paul Peterson. He wrote a wonderful editorial column." Oliver looked pensive for a moment and then it clicked.

"I've read his columns, reprinted in other papers. I think we even ran his editorials a few times. His analyses of European politics and the war were brilliant." She looked proud when he said it. "You'll have to send me his recent ones when you go back."

"He's not writing now," she said quietly, as Oliver looked at her strangely.

"Why not?"

"He died of the flu in December."

"What does that mean for you, Alex? Are you alone in this country now?" More than that, she was alone in the world, but he didn't realize that she had no living relatives left in Europe either.

"Yes," she answered his question simply.

"What will you do when you graduate?" It was three years away, so she had time to decide.

"I'm trying to figure that out. I think I'd like to get a job in New York. Maybe here."

"The only department they'd hire you for is Society, where you are now. You don't want to be writing about weddings for the rest of your life."

"I might have to. It's a start."

"That's what I did with Crime. And then you get stuck. They don't pay you enough so you can afford to give up the job. I want to write a book one of these days. I'm saving all my money for that. I want to leave here in the next year or two, and write a novel. I've seen enough dead bodies for one career. It's a sick way to make a living," he said somberly.

They talked about Europe then. He had loved his time in England, and he had been to France with his mother as a child, which made her think that his family had had money then. Alex and Oliver were in somewhat similar circumstances, with no family, and only burning ambitions. But she guessed that her financial circumstances were far better than his. She owned a newspaper, which she couldn't tell him.

He liked her even better after lunch than before, now that he knew more about her. He felt bad that she had no relatives in the States, since her grandfather had died. He knew what that was like, and she was a woman, and only nineteen years old. She was incredibly naïve—anyone could see it. Talking to her made him want to protect her, but she seemed to be doing fine on her own. And she had very definite ideas. He had noticed during lunch that when he pushed too hard on a subject she didn't agree with, she didn't become aggressive, she just pulled back, and took another path to reach the same goal, but she never lost sight of it, and she didn't give up. She had perseverance. He liked her combination of gentleness and strength—she remained feminine at all times, but she was a very strong woman, who knew her mind, and what she believed in. She had no doubts.

As they left the cafeteria, he said she'd have to come and visit the Crime office sometime, some evening when it wasn't too busy.

"They play cards all day, waiting to get sent out on assignments. We're either rushing like maniacs, or sitting around waiting. The guys love to play poker. Do you play?" he asked her.

"I play cards, but not poker."

"It's easy. I'll teach you sometime."

There were a lot of things he wanted to do with her now, and to show her. He wanted to take her under his wing and protect her. He rarely had weekends off, but he would have loved to take her out for a nice dinner. He loved her company, and talking to her, but he didn't want to date her. He knew it would get complicated. He was seventeen years older than she, and he knew his own difficult nature and fear of relationships. He didn't want to start something he couldn't finish. He meant it when he said he would never marry. He didn't want to break his child's heart if the marriage didn't work out, the way his father had broken his when he left. Oliver thought a serious relationship was the first step to disaster and an accident waiting to happen. He didn't want to break Alex's heart, or have her break his, and she was so breathtakingly beautiful that he was sure they would lose control once they started and head straight into a wall. He didn't want that for either of them. She wasn't the kind of girl one could have a fling with. She was the genuine article. She was solid gold.

He looked wistful when she thanked him for lunch and left him to go back to her office, and he walked to his desk with a serious expression. There was no point starting something with her, he told himself, she was leaving in less than two months. He could think of a dozen reasons not to pursue her, but he wanted to anyway.

He was sent out on one of the Gambino court appearances after that. They were always bringing the Gambinos in for something, and they would appear with their fleet of lawyers, pull all the right strings, and the charges would get dropped. Today was more of the same. Oliver sat in court, thinking about Alex, wishing that things were different and she worked in New York, and had a normal life with a normal family. She was so vulnerable that he was afraid to touch her and ruin her life. He had nothing to give her, and she had suffered enough and he didn't want to add to it. He knew that if he let himself get close to her, he would hurt her in the end. That was the last thing he wanted for her. Or for himself. She was someone to stay away from, no matter how appealing she was.

Alex was pensive too when she went back to her office after lunch with Oliver. All she wanted to do was take away the pain of his past. And she had no idea how. The scene he had described of his mother's death made her heart ache for him.

Alex had been following the activities of the National Women's Party since she'd started school in Chicago. She had attended a few meetings. But once the Nineteenth Amendment had been passed by the Senate, there were fewer meetings. It was up to the individual states to enforce the new law and see that it was respected. There was a smaller sub-group that held meetings to increase women's wages and inform them of their rights. She had read that they were planning to hold a peaceful rally two days after her second lunch with Oliver.

She hadn't seen him since their lunch, and she'd been planning to ask him what he thought of the rally, but had forgotten to mention it at lunch. The rally was going to be held near the factories in the garment district where women were working for shockingly low wages, sometimes working eighteen-hour days in terrible conditions. The rally wasn't too far from her hotel, in the West Thirties, and she was tempted to go, just to show support. She didn't want to ask the girls in the office to go with her, and risk getting accused of being a troublemaker and getting fired. She was enjoying her job and didn't want to lose it. But she was curious about the rally.

It was on Friday night and she had nothing to do. She decided to walk from her hotel in Murray Hill, and observe for a few minutes. It was due to start at eight o'clock, and she didn't plan to stay long.

She was surprised to find when she got there that it was a bigger group than she'd expected, and of many nationalities. Many seemed to be speaking Polish, German, or Yiddish. They were seamstresses in the factories around them. And there was a large Asian contingent, conversing loudly in Chinese. They all were a noisy group, and less well-behaved than the meetings and rallies Alex had attended for the vote. There was very little English spoken in the crowd, and most of the women were strident and angry right from the beginning. Their anger was justifiably directed at the factory owners, but as there were none present, they began pushing and shoving and arguing between the various factions. Within minutes the gathering turned into a seething mass of angry, frustrated women fighting with each other rather than their oppressors, and Alex realized that the wisest course was to leave as quickly as possible. But it was too late. When Alex turned to leave, she found that more women had arrived behind her and she couldn't move in the crowd. She was trapped, and was trying to avoid the punches and blows the women were landing on each other. Some of them were very powerful, and she got two sound blows to the head from women bigger than she was. She wasn't sure if there was normally this much hostility between European and Asian women, and she couldn't understand what they were saying. In their rage, they began turning over garbage cans, and using the lids to smash windows and damage cars or hit each other.

The fighting became increasingly vicious and there was nothing Alex could do to get out and escape them. They were pulling each other's hair, and brawling in the street. People were hanging out the upper windows of residential buildings to watch them fight. It was a poor neighborhood that was mostly industrial, but some people lived there too, in slum conditions. Some of the women in the apartments came downstairs to join the fray. It seemed like senseless violence to Alex and she was sorry she had come. She covered her head with her arms as best she could, and was buffeted by the crowd like a cork in the ocean.

The police arrived quickly, and pushed the women with their clubs. The women attacked them too, and the police got rough with them. Wagons arrived, and the cops began pushing the women into them to arrest them. Many of the women fled then, but there were well over a hundred left on the street, and Alex was among them, still at the center of the action, with women swinging at each other and at the police. Alex was eager to get close enough to a police officer to ask for his help to get her out of the crowd. She had come in simple clothes not to attract attention, a cotton skirt, sandals, and a blouse. There was nothing to distinguish her from the crowd of rough women who were still swinging at each other and the cops. The police kept trying to separate them from each other and then the women would attack the police. It was a genuine brawl worthy of any mob of drunken men. The women weren't even drunk—they were irate and crazed and had exploded.

A big burly Irish policeman finally got close enough for Alex to ask for help, but before she could speak, he had grabbed her by the neck, lifted her off the ground by the shoulders, and thrown her into one of the wagons, on top of the other women, with a fresh heap of women who landed shortly after, crushing Alex beneath them until she could barely breathe, and when the wagon was full, they were taken off to the police station to be arrested. Alex had to fight for air all the way there. Once arrived at jail, they were all pulled out of the wagons and dumped unceremoniously on the sidewalk, then pushed into the police station with the use of clubs again. It was obvious that the men in uniform were utterly fed up with them. Blows rained on the officers from the women pummeling them. The women were the most unruly group Alex had ever seen, and when she tried to stand up, she found that she had injured her ankle and couldn't walk. The police and the crowd shoved her along into the building, and she grabbed onto a police officer before she fell over.

"Please help me, I got caught in the crowd. I'm not part of this. I'm hurt, can you please take me home?" He looked at her as though she was crazy and pushed her back into the herd of women still flailing and shouting, and she discovered that somewhere in the fray, on the street or in the wagon, her purse had disappeared off her arm, perhaps with a broken strap, and she could show them no identification. She had nothing else with her. She tried to reach out to another officer, who ignored her and pushed her away. The police shoved them all into holding cells, and four more wagons arrived before they stopped coming. The women were screaming and fighting and arguing again by then, and causing mayhem in the cells. By then, Alex's arm was hurting, her head was pounding, she couldn't stand on one foot, her lip was swollen, and she thought she might have a black eye. And she was being arrested.

A police officer walked up and down in front of the overcrowded holding cells and told them their situation. They were arrested, and were going to be booked. They could release themselves for the fee of ten dollars, or they would spend two days in jail. Since most of them didn't speak English, they went on screaming and shouting and crying. Alex reached through the bars then, and grabbed the sleeve of an officer, and tried to sound as sane and respectable as she could.

"I'm Alexandra Bouvier," she said urgently, "I'm here from Chicago, I got caught in this mob on the street, I am not part of it. I've lost my purse. May I please call my brother to come and get me? I'm injured." She hadn't even noticed that one sleeve of her blouse was torn.

"He'll have to pay your fine to release you." The officer observed her closely, and the way she spoke to him suggested that she might be telling the truth.

She didn't know anyone to call, but Oliver had given her his phone number to call if she ever had a problem. He said it was a phone in the hall of his building, he didn't have his own. She remembered the number, it was a simple one. A minute later, the policeman pulled her out of the holding cell, while pushing the others back. She hobbled to the sergeant's desk, following him, and he pointed to the phone.

"You have two minutes," he said in a heavy Irish brogue, "or you're here for two days." She dialed the number with shaking hands. A voice answered finally, and she asked for Oliver in a breathless voice. She wondered if he might be working, but he came on the line two minutes later, while the police chatted with each other. She spoke to Oliver as quickly as she could.

"I'm really sorry. I need help. I'm in jail. Can you bail me out? It's ten dollars. I'll pay you back."

"You *what*?" he said in disbelief. She sounded frantic so he knew it was real.

"I've been arrested. I need your help. They want ten dollars to bail me out. Can you come?"

"Where are you?" She leaned toward the two police officers to ask.

"Where am I?" They gave her the address and she told Oliver, and one of the two cops turned to her.

"Your time is up," he said sternly, and he took the phone from her, pushed her back toward the holding cell, opened the door, and shoved her in. She stood there, feeling like a criminal, praying that Oliver would show up. It was mortifying, but she had no one else to call.

Twenty minutes later, a different officer stood in front of the long wall of holding cells that contained the prisoners and shouted her name above the din.

Alex waved frantically until he saw her, unlocked the door, and pulled her out, and she limped out of the jail behind him into a large room where people were waiting, reporting crimes, and explaining their mundane problems to a sergeant at a desk. Oliver was standing in the middle of the room and stared at her in disbelief as she limped toward him, in genuine pain from her ankle. She looked like she'd been hit by a bus.

"What in God's name happened to you? Were you attacked?" He would have laughed at her but she looked pathetic, and she was hurt. He had come as quickly as he could. "You said you were arrested." She looked like she'd been in a brawl with ten men. Worse, she had been mauled by a hundred women.

"I thought it was an NWP rally for better wages," she said, as tears filled her eyes as he put an arm around her shoulders to support her and led her out of the station. "They went crazy, attacking each other, beating each other up, breaking things. The police came, and they attacked them, and I got caught in the middle, and then they threw us into wagons and arrested us." He had kept his cab waiting and gently helped her into it, and gave the driver his address. "Where are we going?" she asked him, as he dried her cheeks gently with his handkerchief and the tears rolled down her cheeks. She was mortified, and scared, and her ankle was excruciatingly painful, and so was her head.

"We're going to my apartment to clean you up. You can't go back to your hotel looking like that," he said, trying not to smile. The situation was so absurd, and the kind of thing a young innocent girl could get herself into. One sleeve of her blouse had been completely torn off. He was eyeing her injuries and he thought they were superficial. "Do you think you need a doctor?" She shook her head and blew her nose on the handkerchief he gave her.

"I'm so sorry. I didn't know who to call," she said, feeling pathetic and embarrassed to have him see her that way.

"I'm glad you called me." He looked at her closely. "I think you're going to have a hell of a shiner tomorrow." Fortunately she had the weekend for the minor injuries to fade. He wasn't sure about the ankle, and hoped it wasn't broken. She cried more on the drive to his apartment and told him the whole story. He carried her up the stairs when they got there and deposited her on a worn brown leather couch. The apartment looked cozy and masculine and he took her to the bathroom to wash her face, and went to make her a cup of tea. He handed her a bathrobe for her to wear until he figured out what she could wear to go home.

She emerged from the bathroom in his robe, looking calmer.

She had a small cut above her ear from one of the garbage can lids, and he was right, she had a black eye and a swollen lip, but there was no other visible damage, just the headache and the ankle. He handed her some ice wrapped in a towel for her lip and eye, and another towel with ice for her ankle, put some pillows behind her on the couch, and sat in a big leather chair next to her and held her hand.

"That will teach you to play rough with a bunch of girls in a bar fight," he said, and she laughed. She looked infinitely better than she had when they arrived. She'd been frightened more than anything.

"I told the police you were my brother," she said, still embarrassed.

"At least you didn't say I'm your father. This brings back memories. I haven't been called to bail anyone out of jail since college. How on earth could you go to that street brawl?" he asked her, half amused and half worried. The ankle was very swollen and bruised, and she winced when he touched it. She said the ice was helping.

"I thought it would be a peaceful demonstration for higher wages and I wanted to help. None of them spoke English and they behaved like savages."

"The factories don't hire them out of finishing schools. May I extract a promise from you, Miss Bouvier?" he said seriously, and she nodded. She still looked pale and badly shaken. "Two promises," he corrected. "One, that you will always call me if you need help. You did the right thing. And two, that you will not go to any more rallies or riots or demonstrations. Especially not here. This is a rough city. It's not some farm town in Illinois. And you shouldn't do this in Chicago either. The Mafia families are making Chicago extremely dangerous now too. Will you promise?"

"I promise," she said solemnly. They talked for a while, and then he gave her one of his clean shirts to wear with her skirt, and he took her back to her hotel. She used his hairbrush to get her hair in order, and she looked respectable enough when they left his apartment and he carried her to the cab. She could step gingerly on her foot by then, and Oliver thought it was a bad sprain, but not broken.

He had his arm around her in the cab on the drive home, and she closed her eyes and leaned her head against his shoulder. As he looked down at her with a tenderness she didn't see, his heart was aching for her. She was so sweet and so young and innocent, and so alone. He could feel himself being swept away on a wave of feelings for her that he had sworn he wouldn't allow himself to feel. She was impossible to resist, but he knew he'd have to try. She had climbed right over his carefully built walls and into his heart. It frightened him more than the street brawl she'd been in, or anything in the world. Love was a risk he never allowed himself to take.

Chapter 10

A bouquet of pink roses arrived at the hotel for Alex on Saturday from Oliver. He debated about sending them, but he felt sorry for her. He didn't call, because he didn't want her to have to come down to the lobby to speak to him on the phone, with her injured ankle. He had added to his note with the flowers "Cafeteria Monday at 1."

By the time she went to work on Monday, all the minor bruises had faded, and the small cut above her ear didn't show. She was limping, but she could walk, and she put makeup on the eye and wore dark glasses. She told everyone she'd tripped and fallen down the stairs at her hotel.

She met Oliver at the cafeteria at one for lunch. He was relieved to see her looking so much better, and she apologized profusely, for calling him and for getting herself into such a mess.

"I've never been arrested before," she whispered, and he laughed.

"That's comforting to know. You remind me of why I never wanted children. I don't want to be bailing them out of jail in my sunset years." Alex felt foolish more than anything else. In Chicago, she could have called someone at her grandfather's newspaper, although she would have been in disgrace. But she knew no one she could call in New York, except him. "Happy to be of service."

Their friendship had taken a giant leap forward after his rescuing her and seeing her in such disarray. She felt completely at ease with him, and he felt closer and protective of her. She wasn't dangerous as he had feared, just young and naïve. And her innocence was endearing.

She had to work late one night that week that he would be on duty too, and he told her to stop by at the reporters' room if she had time. He wanted to see more of her, but wouldn't allow himself to. He didn't want to start something he couldn't finish. And in six weeks she'd be leaving New York. He was aware of it each time he saw her. He was as vulnerable as she was, and alone. She had no idea of her effect on him, and told herself they were just friends. She had never been in love, and didn't recognize the signs. He did, and was poised for flight, to preserve his safe little life behind high walls. No one had succeeded in climbing over them since he built them years before. They had served him well so far. But Alex was undaunted by his walls.

Tommy had seen them leaving the cafeteria after lunch on Monday, and whispered a warning when he saw Oliver at his desk. "Watch out for the young ones, Ollie. They're heartbreakers. Even the nice ones like your little princess from upstairs.

Once you get caught in their net, you're dead." But Oliver knew it too. He was seventeen years older than Alex, and she had her whole life ahead of her, three more years of school, and no family. If he opened his heart to her, he'd feel responsible for her and never leave. There was no way a romance could work between them, and he didn't want to try.

She had to work on the layouts from a big party, with Pam MacDonald, and had agreed to work late. Alex stuck with it, under Pam's close supervision, and she was finished by eight o'clock, and stopped in the Crime department reporters' room before she left the building. Oliver's face lit up when he saw her. He constantly gave her conflicting messages at the same time, to come closer and to stay away. It confused her, but she thought it was just how he was. He had been through a lot in his lifetime too, and she had deep scars.

When she came to the Crime room, he led her to a much smaller back room. He opened it and there was a table with five men around it, and a thick cloud of smoke hanging over the table. Sam and Tommy were there, and three other reporters she had seen but didn't know. They were playing poker, and having fun, waiting to be sent out on a call.

Oliver had them deal him in, and took a chair, he put another chair next to him, and invited Alex to sit down. He explained to her what he was doing and she picked it up quickly. The men loved having her there. She was wonderful to look at and fun to be with. She had all the energy and excitement of youth. She stayed with them, watching the game and learning, until they finally got assigned and had to go out at midnight. The police had called them. She left when they did and went to her hotel, after a very entertaining evening. Tommy teased Oliver as they drove to the crime scene.

"You're a goner, my boy," he said to Oliver in the car. They had a photographer with them in the back seat and Tommy was driving. "She's a terrific girl. You could do worse."

"She's too young, and I'm too old, and it's too late for me. She needs someone her own age. I'm going to tell her that when she leaves," Oliver said, staring out the window and thinking of her.

"You'll be sorry you did, if you tell her that. And you're not too old. It's never too late. I'd snap her up in a minute, if I had the chance," Tommy said as they arrived at the crime scene. There was a body with a tarp over it on the ground, and a pool of blood they could see from the car.

"Lucky for me you don't have the chance," Oliver said with a grin, and they got out of the car and headed for work. The pool of blood was a familiar sight to them, and just another night's work.

Oliver and Alex continued to see each other for lunch at the cafeteria once or twice a week. He took her to dinner at some of his favorite haunts. They went to the beach on Long Island on a Saturday in August when he didn't have to work, and the rest of the time, she enjoyed the wonders of New York. He teased her about the rally occasionally. He was just grateful she hadn't been injured more severely. On her last night in New York, they had dinner together. All three of her bosses had given her glowing references. And there was a lunch for her at the office on her last day of work. The two months of her internship had raced by, and Oliver was sad to see her leave. He was used to her now, and they confided in each other like old friends. There was always an undercurrent of something more, which Oliver did everything possible to ignore. He was intent on remaining just friends until she left.

"Will I hear from you?" she asked softly, and he smiled, fighting back everything he felt for her. He was part brother, part father, part best friend. He was everything she no longer had in her life, a confidante, an advisor, a protector, and she was the same to him. She was like a benevolent fairy at the edge of his life. He knew he would miss her acutely, but he had to get used to life without her again. She was everything he had sworn he would never allow into his life, but it was already too late and he knew it. She owned his heart, but he didn't want her to know, and he was determined not to let his feelings show. He had succeeded so far.

"You probably won't hear from me," he said honestly. "I don't like writing letters. I don't have a phone at home, and neither do you, except one in the dorm."

"You'll have to come to Chicago then," she said, teasing him, but she was sad to leave too. She couldn't imagine life without him now after being so close. She could sense that whenever she came too close to him, he retreated behind his walls. When he let his guard down, he disappeared for a day or two afterward to regain some distance. She didn't know if she'd ever see him again, but it seemed unlikely. She realized she might not. She knew by then that she loved him, but she had no idea how he felt about her, and yet he was always there, looked for her, had lunch with her, and they enjoyed and confided in each other. They had shared their deepest secrets, and talked about the books they both wanted to write.

"I think I might start my book now," he said at dinner that night. He knew it would keep him busy and his mind off of her.

"Chicago is not very far, you know," she reminded him, and he nodded with a pensive look.

She had survived so many agonizing losses and he such brutal ones in his youth, they were both afraid of loving again, and losing one more person. Alex wasn't sure she could bear it, so she didn't press him or try to hang on. He looked closely at her when he took her back to her hotel. They were standing a little distance from the entrance, as he gazed down at her. She was taking the train to Chicago in the morning. She was going to spend a week at home before school started.

"I'm going to miss you terribly," she said softly, in a voice hoarse with emotion she couldn't control.

"I forbid you to miss me," he said with a smile. "I won't miss you at all," he teased her. And then without a word, he kissed her, as he had wanted to since the day he met her and wouldn't allow himself. He wanted one kiss to remember her by. He was sure he would never see her again, and believed it was better that way, for both of them.

"I love you, Oliver," she said softly after he kissed her and continued to hold her. He didn't want to let go, but he was forcing himself to set her free.

"Don't," he said in a whisper. "It would be a terrible mistake." So was losing each other, but she didn't say it. She couldn't force him to love her, or see her again. She gently brushed his lips with hers, and then walked into the hotel. She turned once to see him, and his eyes were riveted to hers. He wanted to remember every minute with her, and then he put his head down, turned and walked away. They were the best two months of her life, and leaving him was one of the hardest things she'd ever done. But she knew she had to respect who he was. He was a man who had watched his mother die in front of him, under the ice. She wasn't sure he would ever be able to love again. He firmly believed that he could not, he couldn't allow himself to, in case it happened again, and he lost someone he loved.

The week Alex spent in Beardstown after New York was peaceful and full of tender memories of her grandfather. She visited the paper, which was hard because it reminded her so much of him, even more than his home. She spent time with Josiah Webster, and told him about her internship. They talked about the pandemic, which had mysteriously disappeared over the summer. Five hundred million people had been affected around the world. Somewhere between fifty and one hundred million people had died, including both her grandparents. After a year and a half, the flu had simply vanished.

As Alex prepared to go back to school in Chicago, she had to get used to life without Oliver. She didn't try to call him or write to him. She knew that if she ever spoke to him again, it would have to come from him. And he didn't seem to be capable of it, nor want to be.

School began a week after she got back from New York. Yoko, her roommate, had transferred to a small college in San Francisco to be close to her widowed mother, and Alex was assigned a room alone for her sophomore year. She liked her classes, and wrote in her journal.

She reported to her literature instructor how much she had enjoyed her internship, and thanked him. She had made no close friends at the university. Her only close friend had been Oliver and now he was gone.

She was startled in November when a girl she knew from the dorm and one of her classes invited her to her debut ball in New York. They hardly knew each other, and the girl explained to Alex that she was supposed to come out the year before, but it had been canceled due to the Spanish flu. With the pandemic over now, the deb ball had been reinstated and she hoped Alex would come.

"I'd love it if you would. I know it's a long way to go for a party." It was happening the week before Christmas, and Alex dreaded the holidays now with no family to celebrate with, so it would be a good distraction from family-oriented events that were too painful for her now.

She accepted the invitation and went shopping for a dress at

Marshall Field's. She hadn't worn an evening gown since the crossing from Paris to New York, when she moved to Beardstown to live with her grandfather. She was almost two years older now, and she looked more grown-up. She bought a brushed silver gown with shoes to match, and reserved a room at the Martha Washington Hotel in New York where she had spent the summer. She hadn't heard a word from Oliver since the night before she left when he kissed her. She knew she wouldn't hear from him. He didn't have the strength or the courage to love again. She didn't know if she did either, which was part of why she didn't press him and hadn't contacted him and had let him go.

The trip to New York was familiar to her now, and she liked spending the night on the train.

New York had a festive air when she got there. Store windows were decorated for Christmas. There were Christmas trees up in public places, and one in the lobby of her hotel. It gave her a thrill to know that she was in the same city as Oliver. She wanted to see him, but she was afraid to call him. He might refuse to see her, or even take the call. He had sought no contact with her in four months, since August. She was going to call him, but she couldn't decide when. It was embarrassingly frivolous to come to New York for a party, but the deb ball was a big deal to her friend. She was sure that the paper must be covering it. She hadn't called Sylvia Bates either, and the prospect of seeing Oliver when she was in town had made the decision for her. She needed no other reason to go.

The ball was on Friday night. She didn't expect to know anyone there. She felt very brave walking in alone, and five minutes after she got there, she ran into Sylvia, who was excited to see her and had Alex pose for a photograph for the paper.

"Are you coming back to us next summer?" Alex had been debating about it, and hadn't applied for a summer job yet, but seeing Sylvia brought it all back and made it seem appealing. She wasn't sure how Oliver would feel about it, if he would think she was chasing him. "We want you back," Sylvia insisted before she went to photograph the debutantes with their escorts.

Alex was seated at a table of young people her age. She was next to a boy who was attending Harvard. None of the girls were in college, and he was impressed that Alex was attending the University of Chicago. They had a lively conversation before the presentation of the debs, and after that he invited Alex to dance. It reminded her of Oliver telling her she should go out with boys her own age. The Harvard junior was very attractive but he seemed like a boy to her. He met up with his friends after he danced with Alex and got dead drunk, and fell asleep on a couch halfway through the evening. The boys her age seemed like children to her, even dressed in white tie for the evening. It wasn't the same thing as her conversations with Oliver about writing, or the fun they had spending time together.

She went home alone, and hung up the silver dress. She finally got up the courage to call Oliver in the Crime reporters' room on Saturday morning. Someone she didn't know answered the phone and she wondered if he had the weekend off. She waited while they looked for him, and suddenly she heard his voice. It was like a bolt of lightning the minute she heard him.

For an instant she didn't know what to say. He sounded busy and distracted, and Alex felt breathless.

"Hello," she said, trying to sound casual and cheerful. "Merry Christmas."

"Alex?" He sounded shocked. "Where are you?"

"I'm in New York. Believe it or not, I came for a deb ball, for a girl I go to school with. How are you?"

"Okay," he said, and then he couldn't stop himself. "Can I see you? Or are you too fancy to see an old hack reporter?"

"You're neither old nor a hack, and I'm no fancier than the night I got arrested," she said, and he laughed, and suddenly it all clicked into place again.

"Have lunch with me. I'll meet you at the deli. I'm stuck here till six tonight." He sounded excited to see her, and she felt a wave of relief wash over her. It was as though she had never left. It all picked up where it left off. She had found him again. She had thought he was lost forever.

She dressed in a warm plaid skirt and navy blue sweater with a heavy coat over it. He was standing on the sidewalk waiting for her when she got there, pacing impatiently to keep warm, and as soon as she stepped out of the cab, he hugged her tight. He looked wonderful and happy. They talked all through lunch about work, school, the book he was writing. He was excited about it. He had started it when she left. He was so happy to see her that it seemed hard to believe he hadn't contacted her since August. He was a man of contradictions and complexities. She was the forbidden fruit he wouldn't allow himself to partake of, for fear of loving her and losing her later. Or loving her too much. He was the mirror of her own fears for the same reasons. They had endured too much loss, but they were braver when they were together than when they were apart. He made her happy and she did the same for him.

"What are you doing about the internship next summer?" he asked her. "Are you coming back? I saw Sylvia Bates at our Christmas party at the paper. She's hoping you will."

"I didn't know she wanted me to until I ran into her last night at the deb ball."

"So will you?" She hesitated, looking at him.

"What do you think about it? What do *you* want?" she asked, hoping to flush him out, but he didn't take the bait.

"I'd love it if you were here." She wanted to ask him why since he hadn't written to her or called her, and had warned her he wouldn't. She was some kind of security blanket for him. It was hard having him act like he was close to her in some ways, and not others. It was more than a friendship. There was the searing kiss the night before she left the last time. It was crazy and confusing, but she didn't have anyone else. He got to that as he paid the check. "So are you dating anyone at school?" he asked bluntly. "Any handsome boys in your classes?" He smiled when he asked her.

"No, to both questions. What about you?" He looked startled by the question, as though it was absurd.

"Of course not. No one can put up with me . . . except you."

"Well, that's interesting. I think you're very easy to put up with. And you've never gotten arrested in the time I've known you. I did," she reminded him, and he laughed again.

"You're the only woman I've ever bailed out of jail."

"You must know very boring women, with no imagination whatsoever."

"So will you reapply for the internship?"

"Maybe I will," she said noncommittally.

"When are you going back to Chicago?"

"Tomorrow, unless you give me a reason to stay." She felt very bold saying that to him.

"I won't," he said confidently. He felt safe enough to be himself with her. "Will you have dinner with me tonight?" he asked her.

"I'd love to," was her quiet response. Whatever this was, it was the relationship they shared, that they had and that seemed to work. He didn't want more. She was disappointed he didn't.

"I'll pick you up at your hotel at seven."

"What'll I wear?"

"Whatever you want." He smiled at her. He looked like a happy man when he left her outside the deli and walked back to work. She did some shopping, and was ready when he picked her up at her hotel that night. She was wearing a simple black dress under her heavy coat, and he took her to Lombardi's pizzeria in Little Italy, which she had loved before.

They talked about his book during dinner, and he encouraged her to do the same. She didn't feel ready and she didn't have any ideas for a book yet.

"I've been thinking," he said carefully, "if I finish the book, and sell it for decent money, I might quit the paper, and just write full-time."

She was surprised. "If I apply for the internship next summer, please try not to quit before I get back." He laughed.

"I promise. Quitting the paper is a long-term thought, not anything immediate."

"Can I play poker with you and the boys if I come back?" she asked. He laughed and nodded.

"That's up to them. I'd love it. They play more often than I do."

He took her back to the hotel, and he confused her again. He pulled her into his arms and kissed her. They stood in the cold for a long time, kissing.

"Will I hear from you before I come back?" she asked him afterward, and he smiled mysteriously.

"No," he said, and she laughed.

"You're hopeless. Maybe that's why I love you." But he was excited now about having two months with her in the summer. He loved having her around for long conversations and meals together, even if he was afraid of more.

As he walked her to the door of the hotel, she stopped and looked at him. "Are you serious that I won't hear from you now until next summer?"

"Maybe . . . I don't know . . ." He looked confused. "I'll think about it," he said, and she kissed him again and ran into the hotel. The best part of Christmas was seeing Oliver in New York. The rest didn't matter to her now. She had no one to spend it with. And she was going to accept a summer job in New York. She would see him again in six months.

Chapter 11

The biggest news item of 1920 was the announcement in January of Prohibition, banning the manufacture, transportation, and sale of alcohol. It created a whole new culture overnight of the pursuit of illegal booze. Prices skyrocketed. Whole networks were created for the clandestine sale of alcohol. Speakeasies sprang up and became glamorous spots to eat, drink, and dance. The Mafia families created a new underworld that brought them a fortune. If anything, people bought and drank more alcohol than ever before.

Oliver wasn't quite as elusive after he saw Alex in December as he had been when she had left in August. He didn't call her often, but he called her every few weeks or sent her a telegram, which he preferred. Neither of their phone situations was ideal, since she had to use the common one in the dorm, and he had to call from a room full of reporters who heard every word he said. In a telegram, he could tell her that he missed her, and couldn't wait to see her in June. But he made no effort to see her before that. He was reinforcing his walls so he could resume their chaste friendship in the summer. Saying that he missed her was a major admission from him, which touched her. And he hadn't completely shut down again. She had gotten under his skin again in December, and reawakened his feelings for her, although he didn't admit it to her, and was still waging war with himself to maintain the distance he needed to feel safe with her.

The time passed quickly with her schoolwork, and she signed up for an accelerated program to begin in September. Starting in the fall, after her internship in New York, she would attend classes for a solid year, without a summer vacation, and she would get her diploma the following fall, and cut the time it took to get it by eight months. It sounded ideal to her.

She had her internship all lined up for that summer, working in the Society office again, with Sylvia as her boss. She promised to give Alex more responsibility and better projects and Alex was looking forward to it. All the same people were working there. It felt like home. And she was getting course credit for the two internships to help her get her diploma faster too. They gave credit to the male students for their internships, and Alex had requested it too. It would be the first time that they had offered the same privilege to a female student. She had negotiated that for herself with the literature professor who liked her, and he could see her point when she asked for what was easily accessible to her male counterparts.

Oliver was filling his time well too. He was working on the novel that had been his dream for years. He worked on it at night, and on his days off. He spent every spare hour on his book, and promised to let Alex read what he had when she got back to New York.

She spent three weeks in June in Beardstown, at the *Courier*. She had meetings with Josiah Webster, so he could explain some improvements he'd made. He was staying abreast of the times, and prided himself on being as modern and efficient as any paper in New York and Chicago. They had won another prize, which would have delighted her grandfather. Paul Peterson had loved his newspaper so much that Josiah and Alex felt it a duty to keep it running the way he would have wanted. He had been far ahead of his time, and Josiah was keeping the *Courier* that way, to honor his old friend.

Oliver was working when Alex arrived in New York. She brought fewer bags and only one trunk, and got to the hotel in the morning. Oliver called her at the hotel after covering a lengthy court appearance of the Bonanno family, over the speakeasies they were running with enormous profits. There had been a shooting at one of them recently and three members of the family had to appear before the grand jury. Oliver knew all of them, and they greeted him like a friend when they saw him in court. The family maintained good relations with members of the press. It was only within the four rival families that violence erupted regularly and bodies in gunny sacks, with blocks of cement tied to them, would turn up in the East and Hudson rivers shortly after. The Bonannos were being charged with violations of the Prohibition laws, not murder this time. They almost always managed to get their family members exonerated and released. They had more attorneys on their payroll than the newspaper did, but they needed them more. They paid off the police at the highest level, as well as all the politicians they could seduce. It was a corrupt world with rich profits that they reaped.

Oliver called Alex from the Martha Washington's lobby afterward and she flew down the stairs to meet him. She hadn't seen him in six months, since December, and she had turned twenty in the meantime. She still seemed like a little girl to him, and he picked her up and spun her around in the lobby, and they went for a long walk over to the East River and sat down on a bench to talk.

She was so happy to see him, she was beaming. She was wearing a pink gingham summer dress, which made her look even younger. He was wearing a suit and tie from work, and looked very handsome and grown-up, sitting next to her on the bench with an arm around her shoulders, enjoying a breeze from the river. She was prettier than ever. Sam and Tommy still referred to her as the Princess.

"How's the book coming?" she asked him.

"Slowly," he said with a sigh. "I keep running into roadblocks with the plot. I don't know why I thought a crime novel was a good idea."

"Because it's what you know and what you love," she said sensibly. It made perfect sense to her. "You can do whatever you want to do," she said, quoting her grandfather, and Oliver smiled.

"Maybe that's why I love you. You always make me feel as

though I can do anything. When I'm working on the book, I'm not so sure."

"It'll come." When she said it, he believed her. Her faith in him was tangible and gave him wings.

They never talked about their future. Alex lived in the present, which suited him. It was the future he was afraid of and didn't trust, based on the past. And Alex was more certain of his future than her own. He believed in her too.

They had dinner at a Chinese restaurant that night, to celebrate her return. She loved being back in New York, although she had come to love Chicago too. It was a small, sophisticated city, with lots of cultural opportunities, beautiful museums, great restaurants, and excellent academic institutions. She wanted Oliver to come and visit her there, but he always said he was too busy, especially now with the book. And the newspaper was full of the increased activities of the five major Mafia families in New York. Prohibition was making them even richer than they already were. They had beautiful estates on Long Island and in New Jersey, and the wives were well dressed and looked more respectable than some of the socialites in the city.

Alex and Oliver walked back to her hotel after dinner, and she loved seeing him again, and being able to talk to him anytime and see him every day.

Alex rapidly discovered that their relationship was no longer a secret when she went back to work the next day. There had been whispers before, and rumors among the Crime team, but now it was common knowledge that Oliver was seeing her. He didn't seem to mind, which was new.

"Should I be planning a layout for a wedding?" Sylvia asked her when she saw Alex in her office, and she blushed and shook her head.

"It's not that serious, and Oliver doesn't believe in marriage, for himself."

"Where does that leave you?" Sylvia looked concerned, although she'd never married and had had the same married lover for twenty-four years. His wife knew and didn't care—his wife just didn't want the embarrassment and inconvenience of a divorce. And Sylvia had accepted it long since. Sylvia took vacations with him, and he spent two nights a week with her. They had a routine that worked for them, but she would have preferred to be a wife and not the mistress.

"It leaves me happy and free," Alex said, smiling.

"At your age, you should have a wedding ring and babies," Sylvia said seriously. She had grown very fond of Alex when she worked for her before.

"I don't need that now," Alex said. "I'm only twenty, and I've never wanted babies. The world is such an uncertain place, I'm not sure I want to bring a child into it." She had lived through a war not so long ago, and a pandemic, and was still marked by them. The world still seemed like a dangerous place to her. She was only just beginning to feel safe again, especially when she was with Oliver. "I don't want to spoil what we have," she said to her boss. Their relationship was easy and light, although Oliver still had his dark moments, and didn't like to talk about it, but she could sense when he was troubled and turned inward. She was certain it was because of his mother's death when he was twelve. She had her own burdens to carry, and her own ghosts from the past. They had that in common. And marriage frightened both of them, and she felt too young to marry.

The time Alex and Oliver shared during her second summer internship brought them even closer than before. They could talk about any subject, enjoyed doing the same things. They loved exploring old junk shops to find treasures, going to art shows, wandering in museums. They both liked to read for hours when he wasn't working. And he let her read the first five chapters of his novel, which was all he had so far, and she thought it was brilliant. He shone like a star when she said it to him. He had faith in her judgment, and her taste in literature was eclectic and profound.

"When are you going to start yours?" he asked her from time to time, just to remind her.

"I don't know. When I'm ready . . . maybe never. I can't get anything on paper whenever I try. I have some ideas, but they're stuck inside me and I can't get them out."

"They'll come out eventually, if you let them," he said gently.

"I'm not sure I can write a book. Maybe all I can do are short stories and my journal. And copy describing weddings." He smiled at that. Sylvia had given her bigger projects this time, but Alex still thought that their society coverage was meaningless, superficial work, and Oliver agreed with her. She was capable of so much more.

"Remember what your grandfather said. You can do anything

you want. Maybe you'll write a book about a bride." She threw an apricot at him when he said it, and he opened it and shared it with her.

"We have wonderful fruit in my grandfather's orchards," she said nostalgically, suddenly thinking of Beardstown in the summer and how lush everything was. "Do you think you'll ever come to see it?" It was her fondest wish, but she knew it was unlikely to happen, and Oliver wouldn't come.

"I'd like to," he said gently, knowing what it meant to her. But to him, visiting her home seemed like a deep symbolic commitment, even if her family wasn't there. It was also why he had never pressed for a physical relationship with her. Because he wasn't willing to marry her if they did and he was an honorable man and respected her. And he knew that if they had sex, she'd be even more attached to him, and expect even more of him, and he couldn't live up to it. He was surprised that she still had her grandfather's house to go to, and that they hadn't sold it when he died. He never questioned her about it. And he knew she still visited the paper where he had worked whenever she was in town. There were still parts of their histories that they kept to themselves.

"Will you come to Chicago this winter?" she asked him, two weeks before she was scheduled to go back. She never pressed him about it, or marriage. He knew she wasn't anxious for it either. She wanted to complete her education first, and have a career. But he could sense that she wanted some kind of commitment from him. He knew he couldn't give it to her and wasn't sure he ever could. He knew what was stopping him, but he had never said it to her.

They were walking down a beach the following weekend, and they sat on the sand side-by-side, looking out to sea.

"I used to think there were mermaids in the sea," she said, snuggling next to him, and he smiled. "My mother said there were and I believed her. She was so beautiful." There were tears in her eyes when he glanced at her, and he pulled her closer. He wanted to protect her from anything that could hurt her, but he couldn't change the past, just as she couldn't change his for him or the scars it had left. They were sitting there quietly with no one else around, far down the beach, when he turned to her and surprised her.

"There's something I haven't told you," Oliver said to her, and she had never seen him look as serious. It frightened her for a moment.

"You're married, and have a wife and ten children?" She tried to lighten the moment and he shook his head.

"I told you that I've never been in love, and that's true. I've never loved anyone as I love you. But I was in love once when I was very young. We were children really. She was seventeen and I was nineteen. We had in common that her father had abandoned her and her mother too. Her father ran off with some young girl. Peggy wasn't a happy person. She didn't get along with her mother. And we didn't get along the way you and I do. She wanted us to run away and get married. I was in college. We had no money. She had a job in the coffee shop where her mother was a waitress. I met her while I was in college, and I wanted to finish school and make something of myself. I told her I couldn't get married yet. It meant everything to her. We fought a lot over it. I knew I wasn't ready. She wanted a baby right away too, which scared me even more. She didn't have a family, so she wanted to make one of her own, and not wait.

"I would have lost my scholarship if I got married. I guess it was selfish of me. I put my needs first, but I knew we could never make a decent life if I gave up college and married and had babies with her, working as a waiter or a gas station attendant. It would have been a disaster." That was obvious to Alex too as he told her the story. "She gave me an ultimatum—run away to Maryland with her and get married, or leave. So I left. Her mother was away for a few days, and she was alone in their apartment. They slept in one bed, it was so small, and I would have had to live with them if we got married. We couldn't have afforded our own place. We fought about it on Saturday morning, and I felt guilty on Sunday. I went back to tell her I'd give up school and we could get married. I thought if she loved me that much, I owed it to her." There were tears rolling down his cheeks as he told her, and Alex listened closely while he did, and held his hand. "When I went back, the door was unlocked and I found her. Peggy had committed suicide. She hanged herself." Alex felt sick as he told her, thinking of what he must have felt like. "She didn't leave a note. She didn't have to. It was my fault because I wouldn't marry her.

"I probably should have ended it with her then, but she was so sweet and young and pretty, although so sad and desperate inside. Her mother never blamed me. She had tried it once, before I knew her." He turned to look at Alex then with a ravaged look. "Do you realize, I've killed two women in my life. I couldn't save my mother under the ice, and I caused Peggy to commit suicide because I wouldn't marry her. I've never loved anyone since and I'm not sure I loved her, not enough to marry her. I've never made a commitment to anyone since, and I probably never will. I never want to drive someone to that point, or disappoint them, or be unable to give them what they need from me. I can't do that to anyone again. It's why I've never talked to you about the future. What if I promise to marry you and then I can't, or don't want to, and something like that happens again?" She could still see easily how traumatized he was by both deaths, and how guilty he felt. He was convinced that he had killed them. Alex put her hands gently on his face and looked into his eyes.

"Ollie, please listen to me. You were a child—there was no way you could pull your mother up through the ice, her clothes were full of water and made her even heavier. I saw something like that happen once in Switzerland. It took three men to pull a woman out. No twelve-year-old boy could do it. And you didn't kill Peggy. There was something wrong in her—you said she'd tried to do it before. She wanted someone else to fix her, and to give her what she didn't have within herself. You can't do that for anyone. You couldn't just give up your whole life for her, and she shouldn't have wanted you to. Some part of her was sick. You couldn't have fixed her." He nodded as she said it but he didn't look sure. All he could remember was Peggy's face when he found her hanging from a rafter. "And I understand how you feel now," she said, desperately sad for him and the weight he was carrying, "but it wasn't your fault." What she said had the ring of truth and he almost believed her.

"You never ask me for anything, or any kind of commitment," he said quietly, "but I know you want that from me, and I'm too afraid. What if I kill you too?"

"You're not going to kill me, Ollie. You can't unless you take a gun out and shoot me. I'm afraid of a commitment too, because if you commit yourself to me, what if it kills *you*? Everyone I've ever loved has died. All of them. My parents, my grandparents. I had a crush on a boy when I was sixteen. He got drafted when he turned eighteen and he was killed in the war. I barely even loved him, and he died too. He was a sweet boy. I'm afraid that if you make a commitment to me, or marry me, you'll die too and I couldn't bear it. I'd rather stay like this forever than lose you too." She was crying then too, and he held her tight in his arms and kissed her face drenched in tears. It felt good to be honest with each other, but their memories and their fears were so painful and such heavy burdens for both of them. They were evenly matched.

"I'm not going to die because I marry you, Alex. I won't die because you love me. We've been through a war and a pandemic— millions of people died. You just had the bad luck that the people you loved were among them. That's chance, it's not your destiny. And maybe that's true for me too. Will you believe me?" he asked her seriously.

"No," she said through her tears, and he smiled. "You're probably lying to me just to make me feel better."

"I will *not* die just because we love each other," he repeated. "I swear."

"And there's something I haven't told you. It's the only secret I have from you, and I don't want to have any. My grandfather didn't work for a newspaper," she said, and he looked surprised.

"But I've read his editorials. Who wrote them?"

"He did. But he owned the newspaper, he didn't work there. He loved it as much as any child. He left it to me when he died, with good people to run it, so I don't have to be there. But maybe I'll want to run it one day myself. I haven't decided that yet. But I own a newspaper. I'm not an heiress or a debutante. And I'm not rich. But I have some money that he left me too. And a news-paper, and a nice house and a property. I was afraid you wouldn't like me anymore if I told you, or you'd think I was showing off." He looked at her in amazement.

"Why would you think that?"

"You were grumpy about rich people when I met you," she said, and he laughed.

"I'm grumpy about lazy debutantes who don't get an educa-tion, and just want to get married. But that's not you. You study hard, you work hard, and if you run your grandfather's newspa-per one day, I'm sure it will be amazing. Actually, I want to see it," he said, suddenly intrigued by everything she hadn't told him, and she looked enormously relieved.

"So we don't have to ever get married, and you'll live forever, and I'll run the newspaper?" she asked in her childlike way, and he kissed her.

"That is *not* what I said. And who knows, maybe one day I'll force you to marry me, and we can run the newspaper together, between books." She considered what he'd said and looked intrigued by it.

"That might not be so bad," she said with a grin.

"Let's just relax and not worry about it for now," he said, serious again. "Let's see what happens. I won't kill you, and I won't die because you love me, and we don't need to make any decisions. Let's enjoy ourselves for a while, and see where it goes. How does that sound?" he asked her, and she was so young she had years to figure it out.

"It sounds pretty good to me," she said, and he held her in his arms, and then they walked down the beach together, feeling lighthearted and unburdened. He had finally set his ghosts free, and she had told him about the newspaper and her worst fears about his reaction to that. The future was looking much better than it had before. They had let their secrets go. They were free now. They ran through the surf and she splashed him, and they ran back hand in hand to where they'd left the car, and drove back to the city, free of their guilt and burdens. They had no secrets anymore.

Chapter 12

The last two weeks of Alex's summer internship went even faster than the rest. Once they had unburdened themselves of their deepest secrets, she and Oliver felt lighter than air and enjoyed each other even more. Oliver occasionally had trouble controlling his desire for her, but she had no intention of making a mistake, taking a chance and getting pregnant. She was more sensible than he was, most of the time.

"For a man who says he doesn't want children, you're awfully willing to gamble, Oliver Foster," she scolded him, and he apologized.

"You drive me crazy, Alex. I lose my mind sometimes."

"So do I," she admitted. "I just don't want to make a terrible mistake and regret it later."

"I wouldn't, if something like that happened," Oliver said to her. He knew that now. Lately, he had been beginning to warm to the idea of having children with her one day, which was an enormous change for him. He hadn't said anything to her, and he wasn't ready to, but he had been giving it some serious thought. But he also knew that she wasn't ready to have children at her age. She had other plans and dreams to attend to first.

"Speaking of gambling, when can I come and play poker with you, before I leave?" He had taken her to play with them once, and she had won some money. His colleagues loved having her around. She was gorgeous to look at, and a lot of fun. She had had even more fun this time at her job with more responsibilities than she had the year before. And she and Oliver were even more comfortable with each other, especially since they'd made their confessions to each other. They were like two kids sometimes, and he felt like one when he was with her. She had given him back a piece of his youth, and he had done the same for her, as the war and the pandemic faded slowly into the past.

He finally took her to play cards at the paper one night. Technically she wasn't supposed to be in the Crime reporters' room, in case there was confidential information lying around on someone's desk. But they ignored the rules sometimes at night, and the Crime reporters were an unruly group at best, at any hour. Someone had brought in southern fried chicken and ribs that night, and they were helping themselves with paper plates. Alex took some, and they went to play cards in the back room. They'd been playing for about an hour and she had won ten dollars when an alarm went off. The men looked at each other and shrugged and folded their cards and stood up.

"What happened?" she asked them. They were putting their jackets on and stubbing out their cigars.

"Work time for us, Princess. That bell means they need more than one crew. Something big must have happened," Sam said to her. Several phones were ringing and Oliver answered one. He looked serious as he listened, jotted down a quick note. Tommy was on another phone and writing furiously, and they exchanged rapid-fire information when they both hung up. Alex was listening raptly.

There had been shootings in three different locations. There were bodies on the scene. Seven people killed in all, and three injured. Ambulances had already been called and hadn't arrived yet. The police needed two trucks from the morgue.

"It looks like some of the families had a clash tonight. We've been expecting this for a while," Oliver said. He looked alert but unsympathetic. This wasn't a situation where innocent bystanders had gotten hurt, or a natural disaster involving children. This was gangsters jostling each other for large amounts of ill-gotten gains. They were making a fortune from Prohibition and fighting like dogs for it. Oliver had no sympathy for them, and the mess they made was his job to report. All the men who were going chimed in, and suddenly Oliver turned to Alex.

"Do you want to come?" he asked her. "All the shooters are either dead or gone. It will be ugly, but not dangerous." If it were, he wouldn't have suggested it to her. "You can get to see what I do here." She liked the idea, and she wasn't squeamish.

"Will there be guts all over the place?" she asked him, and he shook his head.

Danielle Steel

"The boys from the morgue will get there before we do. You can just wait in the car and watch from the distance if you want, or you can take a cab back to the hotel." But it was exciting to be part of the action. And she was excited to go with him, for a bigger glimpse into his world.

She rode in a car with Oliver, Sam, and Tommy. Four other reporters were in a car going to one of the other locations, and a third team had already left, and photographers had been dispatched to all three locations and were getting into trucks outside. It was going to be a big story the next day.

The men were talking among themselves as Oliver drove, and Alex glanced at him.

"You won't get in trouble for taking me?" she asked.

"No one will know. The boys won't say anything. Every now and then, someone takes a civilian with them. If it looks too rough when we get there, I'll send you home. The cops don't care who we bring with us. There will be a million cops on the scene, and reporters from other papers. A scene like this, involving three of the families, will be buzzing with people coming and going all night. You're probably the first woman who has ever done this though." It felt like an honor to her.

They arrived at the scene minutes later. They were somewhere below Hell's Kitchen, where some of the Mafia operations were. And as Oliver had predicted, it was chaos, but as soon as they reached the epicenter of where the action had happened, he knew he'd made a mistake. Alex was right behind him and hadn't seen anything yet. He stopped her and told her to turn around. The drivers from the morgue hadn't brought enough tarps with

194

them, and there were bodies all over the ground, with gunshot wounds in their heads, half their heads blown off, their brains and entrails spilling on the ground in pools of blood. The photographers were working, two other papers were at the scene, and the police were rushing in and out, directing what they wanted pictures of and trying to identify the victims, since they knew most of them.

To make matters worse, as they were standing outside a warehouse that belonged to one of the families where they received shipments of bootleg liquor, which was what it was all about, it turned out that there was one live shooter left. He came out with guns blazing. A police marksman killed him in two seconds, and there were no other victims. The minute the shooting started, Oliver pulled Alex to the ground and laid his body on top of her. They crawled to a spot behind one of the police cars after that, and waited until the area had been checked again and they were sure there were no other shooters left. Oliver was shaking, realizing what could have happened to Alex. He had been a fool to bring her. He left the scene with her as soon as he was sure it was safe, and hailed a cab for her. He didn't even like sending her home alone from that neighborhood, but he had no other choice.

"I'm sorry, Alex, this was really stupid of me. Lock the car doors and go back to the hotel." He gave the driver a big tip, they took off, and he went back to the crime scene to work.

Tommy gave Oliver a quizzical look. "Did the Princess go home?"

"Yeah. I was insane to bring her. I thought this would be no big deal." Tommy nodded.

"It's always a big deal when these three families are involved."

"I should have known better," Oliver blamed himself. They had all grown blasé and impervious to the violence they saw every day.

They were at the crime site till three A.M., getting the story and the pictures to go with it, with the bodies strewn all over the place, until the morgue finally took them away.

Oliver had a straight scotch when he got home, and he apologized to Alex the next day.

"It was exciting to see what you deal with in a day's work," Alex said, sobered by the experience. "Are you in trouble because of me?" she asked him.

"Probably. I deserve it. I can deal with it. I'm just sorry I exposed you, and scared you, and put you in danger. You could have been shot." He was furious with himself.

He was called up to the managing editor's office that afternoon and given a strong dressing-down. He said that she had brought him something at the office and he didn't have time to take her home, so he had brought her with him, thinking the crime scene was clean. And instead there was another shooter. He admitted his mistake and apologized profusely.

"The next time you pull a stunt like that, you're fired, Foster. Is that clear?" The managing editor didn't mince words. "There are no guests at a crime scene. This isn't a tourist attraction. Can you imagine what her family would have done to us, if she'd been shot or killed?" Oliver didn't tell him that she had no family. That wasn't the point. And his boss was right.

"Perfectly, sir." He took the tongue-lashing like a man because he knew he was guilty. He had a new respect for the work they did, and the men who protected them. And he knew they'd been lucky when the shooter came out of the warehouse. Oliver went back to his office and ran into Tommy on the way to his desk.

"Did you get fired?" he asked Oliver, worried.

"Not this time. And I won't do that again. The shooter could have killed Alex."

"Thank God he didn't," Tommy said, and they both went back to work. It was a huge story, and Oliver had written it for the front page. It had given him another idea for his book, and he exhaled and relaxed, with a powerful lesson learned. If anything had happened to Alex, he would never have forgiven himself.

The girls in Society had given Alex a goodbye lunch that day. Sylvia gave her a scarf that they had all chipped in to buy her. There was a cake, and they were all sorry to see Alex leave. She was sorry too.

"I'll be back," Alex promised, still thinking of the crime scene the night before. She'd been lucky. And she knew she wouldn't be back the following summer, since she'd be in school in the accelerated program till September to get her diploma. But she hoped she'd be back one day. Maybe for a real job and not just as a summer intern. She would like that a lot.

She and Oliver went to dinner at P.J. Clarke's that night. He told her that he'd had a stern lecture from his boss but hadn't gotten fired.

"And it gave me an idea for my book. I needed a scene like

that," he said with a smile. "I'm going to miss you," he told her, and she knew he meant it.

"Will I hear from you this time?" she asked him, but she wasn't as worried as she had been the year before when she left. This year she knew he loved her. She didn't know what they would do about it, or if it would work out, but at that exact moment, she loved him, and he loved her too. And when he left her at her hotel that night and kissed her, it was a kiss she wouldn't forget. They just had to wait and see how things turned out. The one thing she had learned was that you could never predict any-thing, and she didn't try to. Things would happen as they were meant to, in ways they couldn't even begin to guess.

Chapter 13

After the warm summer they'd spent together, Alex was disappointed when she didn't hear from Oliver this time after she left New York. She had felt sure she would. They had gotten so close over the summer, spent so much time together, and shared so many confidences and revelations about their past. She thought he felt comfortable enough to communicate with her now, but he didn't. She didn't hear a word from him from the day she left on the twenty-ninth of August. Not a word or a postcard for the entire month of September, and even into the beginning of October. She had sent a telegram and several letters, none of which he answered. She didn't know if he was working, distracted, writing his book, or if he decided he didn't love her, or couldn't follow through. Anything was possible.

He had said he had a dark side, which she imagined was as a result of his mother's traumatic death and his girlfriend's suicide. He was afraid of commitment, but so was she, and she had asked him for none. He could at least have said hello in some form or other. Instead, there was total radio silence from New York. If nothing else, it seemed unkind. They communicated beautifully when they were together face-to-face, but with any number of miles between them, he turned into a dud. At his age, she thought he could do better and make some slight effort to stay in touch and tell her he loved her. But he made no contact or effort at all. She was annoyed about it as the weeks wore on.

Alex began her accelerated program as soon as she returned from New York, in order to complete her junior and senior years in one twelve-month stretch. She knew it would be intense, but she thought it was worth it, and in the spring, she intended to look in both Chicago and New York for a job for September. She loved both cities. She sent a few cute postcards to Oliver in September, and one funny telegram, to which he didn't respond. Her disappointment and sadness turned to anger at his being cavalier with her.

And in the third week of October, she got a message at her dorm. "Here to do a story. Do you have time for dinner? Staying at The Blackstone. Love, O." Part of her was excited that he had finally surfaced. And part of her was annoyed. It was all a little haphazard if he was there for work and was fitting her in after two months of silence. She wasn't even sure if she wanted to respond or have dinner with him. She finally answered the message and left one at his hotel. "When? Love, A." She wondered if he'd answer her. She was curious about what story he had come to Chicago for.

When she got back from class that day, he was waiting at her dorm. He looked shockingly handsome in a suit and tie, with a well-cut dark blue topcoat. He'd had a haircut, and looked well. She was dressed like a schoolgirl, in a wool skirt and warm coat. Her heart gave a leap as soon as she saw him, and she tried to ignore it. Everything he felt for her was in his eyes. It was hard to deny it. She offered him a cup of tea in the living room at the dorm. There were already three couples visiting there, and one girl with her mother. Oliver suggested a walk. She left her schoolbooks at the front desk and joined him outside.

"What's up?" she asked him, suddenly uncomfortable with him after his long silence. They had been so close when she left New York, and he had put distance between them again by his stubborn silence and not communicating with her.

"Nothing. Why?" he responded. He could see that she was upset, and he knew why. It was his reason for coming to Chicago, to make amends. He hadn't visited her there before. They walked for a little while in silence around the lake, but it was windy and cold. They finally stopped and sat down on a bench, and she shivered in the cold. Winter had come early. "Alex, I know you must be mad at me," he began, and took her hand in his. "I'm sorry I didn't write. I was finishing the book. I finally figured out the end, and I didn't want to stop. I spent every moment I had, when I wasn't working, wrestling with the book."

"You could have sent a postcard, or a telegram. I thought we were past your hiding from me," she said, looking petulant, which he thought only made her look more beautiful, and touched him.

"It was like an express train running through me. I couldn't stop. I worked on the book every night." She'd heard people say that about writing before, but she had never experienced it herself, that burning passion that devoured you. She didn't know if she believed him. Maybe there was another woman in his life. She had thought of everything and now here he was, obviously contrite, but she was angry and hurt. He couldn't just walk in and out of her life like that, but he had. "I get weird about writing to people," he said, still holding her hand.

"Apparently. And if you didn't have this story to do, when would I have heard from you? Next year sometime? What story are you doing?" And she wasn't interning in New York the following summer, since she would be in school in the accelerated program to graduate in Chicago.

"It's about the Gambinos. I used it as an excuse to come and see you. Will you have dinner with me?" He could have warned her but he hadn't.

She didn't answer him at first. "When are you leaving?"

"Tomorrow night. I did the interview today when I got here. I'm free tonight and tomorrow," he said with a pleading look, and then he leaned over and kissed her. He was so tender with her that she melted and felt dizzy when they stopped.

"You really upset me when I didn't hear from you," she said in a small voice, and he pulled her into his arms.

"I don't know what happened to me. Maybe I got scared again. Everything was so good between us when you left, and then suddenly you were gone and I was in the heat of the book. I found an agent," he said with an air of excitement. He had wanted to write a book ever since college and he finally had. It was a major step in his life. "He's a nice guy and he loves it."

"Can I read it?" she asked, excited for him. "You could have sent it to me."

"I brought a copy with me, for you. No one's read it yet but the agent. I want to know what you think." She had made helpful comments before, when he gave her chapters to read, fresh out of his typewriter. She was excited to see it complete. "We should go back to the dorm. I think you're turning blue," he said, and she laughed, as her anger at him dispelled. She loved him and forgave him. She tucked her hand into his arm, and they walked back to the dorm. "Will you have dinner with me?" he asked her again, and she nodded. She hadn't answered him before.

"Yes, I will. But if you disappear like that again, I won't."

"I promise." He had asked at his hotel, and made a reservation at Henrici's, one of the best restaurants in town. He wanted to do something special for her, and celebrate the book. She had encouraged him to do it. And now he had an agent. It was beginning to feel real, and he wanted to share the experience with her, to thank her.

She changed quickly, while he waited in the formal drawing room for guests. She looked beautiful when she walked downstairs in a long black skirt, a little fur jacket, and high heels, with her blond curls piled high on her head. She was dazzling, and he felt proud to be with her. Little by little she relaxed at dinner, and by the time Henrici's famous dessert pastries arrived, they had found their footing again. Not hearing from him had been wounding after telling her he loved her before she left. He was hard to read sometimes, especially when he disappeared.

"How are your classes going?" he asked her.

"The accelerated program is intense, but I'll be done less than a year from now, instead of two years."

"A year is a long time to wait for you to come back to New York." He looked sad when he said it. "I'll miss you next summer," he said, and she smiled ruefully. They both had happy memories of her two internships and the time they spent there.

"I hope you miss me before that," she said ruefully.

"I do—I did for the past two months. I volunteered to do this interview so I had an excuse to come and see you. That's true. I have an idea," he said, wanting to make up to her for upsetting her. "Since the holidays are hard for both of us, why don't I come out here for Thanksgiving? We could have dinner somewhere if you'd like it." Neither of them had families to spend the holiday with. She loved the idea and warmed to it immediately. "I have two days off but I can trade another two with Tommy. His family is on the West Coast and he never celebrates the holidays. He takes them all together once a year."

"I would love it," she said, touched that he would spend the holiday with her. "There's a lot to do here. Theater, ballet, opera, museums," she said with a grateful glance at him.

"I just want to be with you," he said. They were back on track by the end of dinner. And he made the reservation for Thanksgiving dinner before they left the restaurant.

She met him for breakfast at his hotel the next day, and

skipped her classes to spend the day with him. They went to see all the highlights of Chicago. They had lunch together and an early dinner. She took him to the train, and stood on the platform waving after he kissed her and boarded. It felt just like the summer, only better. He waved to her until the train turned a bend and disappeared and she took a cab back to her dorm. His brief visit had restored her faith in him. He was coming back in five weeks. He sent her six telegrams and a steady stream of silly postcards before he returned. He had left the copy of the book with her, and she loved it, and was shocked and touched when she saw that it was dedicated to her.

It said simply, "To Alex, the love of my life, O.F."

She sent him a telegram the morning after she read it that said, "The book is brilliant. All is forgiven, I love you, A."

The five-week wait for him to arrive for Thanksgiving seemed interminable, but with a steady stream of postcards and telegrams from him, she was no longer worried. He had reformed.

She had the most elegant Thanksgiving dinner of her life with him at the Palmer House, and they spent four days exploring every inch of Chicago, and even went to the theater and the ballet. He did everything he could think of to please her. During dinner after the ballet, on his last night, he asked her what she was doing for Christmas. He wanted to invite her to New York. She hated holidays now, because they were so lonely and painful, and then suddenly she had an idea. She didn't know what he would think of it.

"Why don't you come here for Christmas? To Beardstown. You can stay at my grandfather's house. There is always snow on Christmas, it's beautiful there, and we can visit the *Courier*." He hesitated, turning it over in his mind. It was a big step, going home with her for Christmas. But she would be the only one there. There was no family to impress or to have an opinion. It was the kind of thing he never did with women, because it gave them the wrong idea. He never spent holidays with the women he dated, even if it meant staying home alone. But it would be different with Alex. Being with her would make it a real Christmas, for both of them.

"I'd love it," he said, and as he did, he felt all the tension go out of him, and everything he had been fighting for the last three months lifted and vanished. With Alex waiting for him, he felt like he was coming home for Christmas. He hadn't had a real Christmas since he was twelve years old, and the scars had healed at last. He was ready to celebrate his first Christmas with her. She was the first and only person who had soothed his troubled soul.

Chapter 14

It was snowing gently on the day that Oliver stepped off the train in Chicago at ten in the morning. He had taken the Broadway Limited at Pennsylvania Station in New York, and was met at Union Station in Chicago by one of the faithful employees of the *Courier*. Horace, the *Courier* driver, had brought one of their trucks, with a blanket for Oliver, for more warmth than the heat in the truck would provide. He also had a basket of sandwiches that Alex had given him when he left Beardstown at two in the morning, to make sure he met the train on time. Alex didn't expect them back until late that afternoon, so she had provided food and a warm blanket for the trip. There was a thermos of hot coffee in the basket too, and another of hot chocolate.

Horace was waiting on the platform when Oliver stepped off the train and they recognized each other immediately, from Alex's description. A porter carried Oliver's bag to where Horace had parked the *Courier*'s truck, and a light snow was falling.

"The trip is likely to take longer than usual," Horace said after he'd put Oliver's bag in the back, and got behind the wheel. Oliver noticed that the truck was new, in good condition, and immaculately clean. When they left the station, the city looked like a Christmas card, with a light snow coating the lampposts, rooftops, and every surface. It looked like a gingerbread village.

Horace told him that he'd worked for the *Courier* for forty-four years, one of the first people Paul Peterson had hired and visibly proud of it. Oliver smiled as they drove away from the station, which looked like a setting for a model train set. They headed toward Beardstown. Oliver was excited to make the trip, and see the paper and Alex's home. He drank some of the hot chocolate she had sent with Horace, and it was delicious. They talked about the newspaper, Horace's early days working for Paul Peterson, and what a great man he had been. It gave Oliver a new perspective on Alex's history and the family she came from. He had always heard good things about her grandfather, but Horace was a living voice from the past—a personal link to the paper, and Alex's ancestors, and her grandfather's journalistic brilliance and strong moral fiber. It was an interesting history lesson for Oliver.

"I have high hopes for Miss Alex, if she steps into her grandfather's shoes one day," Horace said as he got onto the road that would take them to Beardstown. Oliver couldn't wait to see it now, and the operation at the *Courier* that Alex raved about.

With Horace's sharp eyes and steady hand on the wheel, they reached Beardstown in just under seven hours, in spite of the still-falling snow. Oliver slept part of the way, and it looked like a fairyland when he woke up. They drove past the orchards on the way to the house, which was all lit up, waiting for him. Alex stood in the doorway, having heard the truck approach. The house shone brightly behind her. She was wearing a big white sweater and a red wool skirt, and her hair was a mass of soft curls around her face. Oliver smiled when he saw her. She beamed when she saw Oliver get out of the truck, while Horace got his bag from the back. It was a dream come true seeing Oliver there. She thanked Horace warmly for his important mission bringing Oliver safely home, as Oliver walked up the front steps and followed her into the house.

As soon as the front door closed behind them, he took her in his arms and kissed her. There were delicious smells coming from the kitchen. The housekeeper had made a rich stew that had been simmering for hours, waiting for him to arrive. And looking around at the house she had inherited, he felt like he had come home for the first time since his childhood. She looked more beautiful than ever as she gazed up at him.

He followed her into the big inviting kitchen, which was a combination of state-of-the-art equipment that had fascinated her grandfather, and old-fashioned charm. She poured him a glass of wine and smiled as she handed it to him.

"Welcome to Beardstown, Oliver." She was only sorry she couldn't introduce her grandfather to him. She had a feeling they would have liked each other immensely. Oliver had that feeling too, from everything Horace had said about him. "I'm so happy to have you see all this, especially the paper. My grandfather was so proud of it."

"With good reason, from everything I know of it," Oliver said, taking a sip of the wine.

She turned down the flame under the stew, and they walked into the library, which had an enormous fireplace, three large animal heads—an elk, a moose, and a buffalo—and walls of beautifully bound leather books all around the room. Paul Peterson had an impressive knowledge of and a deep respect for literature and rare books.

"Those are Joey, Charlie, and Francois," she said, pointing to the animal heads. "I named them when I was six." It startled him suddenly to realize that it was a mere fourteen years ago—he had already graduated from college by then, and she was just a child. In some ways, she still was to him, and he loved her openness and innocence, in spite of having come through the war, and lost so many loved ones, including the grandfather who had left her his newspaper and his house. There was never a shred of bitterness or self-pity about her, in spite of her losses, and she was grateful he had come to spend Christmas with her. It was going to be a very different holiday with him there. She had decorated a tree the night before that stood proudly in the front hall. He had seen it on the way in, but didn't realize she'd done it for him. She hadn't had a tree for Christmas since her grandfather died. But she had something to celebrate this year, with Oliver there.

They sat in front of the fire in the library as Oliver got warm.

"I hope the drive wasn't too awful and Horace didn't talk your ear off."

"Not at all. He loved your grandfather, and he has high hopes for you. He's eager for you to run the *Courier* one day."

She looked serious when she answered. "I don't know if I have the skill to ever do that. My grandfather had big shoes to fill. I don't think I could ever measure up to him. He knew so much more than I do."

"You'll learn in time, you've already learned a lot." She'd been very interested in the technical details at the paper in New York. The men in charge of the mechanics had been impressed by her, as well as the editorial staff. Sylvia Bates and her colleagues loved her, and he had heard nothing but good things on the grapevine. But she had her own empire to run one day, if she chose to, which was impressive too. She was still young, but she was hungry to learn all she could. And now he better understood why. Her grandfather's legacy was an important one. She had inherited a newspaper of real quality that had a far reach into the community, and served it well. The *Courier* stood up well to its big-city competition in Chicago. The paper was respected among its peers. Oliver was sorry not to have had the chance to meet Paul Peterson.

The snow continued to fall while they were talking, and they put on coats to walk outside and sit on the porch for a few minutes before dinner.

"I used to love coming here as a child," she reminisced. "I thought it was a magical place. I still do. But I feel like I should be learning everything I can in cities like New York and Chicago. It would break my heart to sell the paper, but I don't know if I'm equal to the task of running it."

"You're up to it. I know you are, Alex," he said gently. "And what you don't know now, you'll learn." He believed it too. The longer he knew her, the more he saw how exceptional she was. And he was glad he had come for Christmas to see this side of her life. Here she wasn't just a summer intern, she was the great hope of the grandfather who had been revered locally, and had kept the farmers abreast of world news while addressing their local concerns. The *Courier* did exactly what it was supposed to. It enlarged their world with solid knowledge and important facts, as well as progress in their field. It was a local paper with a wide-scale, international view.

"I'm not sure they'd respect a woman running it, not the way they did him. He was very special."

"Would your mother have run it if she had survived?" Alex laughed at the idea.

"My mother didn't care about journalism, the only thing she cared about was medicine, just like my father. Nothing else interested them." They were a family of strong passions and brilliant minds, and Alex was no different, Oliver saw easily, and realized again how lucky he was to have found her on his path. He even forgot sometimes that she was French and not American. She adapted to any situation, and had learned a lot about American culture in the three years she'd been there. She fit in wherever she was, with discretion, intelligence, and poise.

She showed him around the house after he poured his second glass of wine. There was a handsome drawing room, which Paul had hardly used since his wife's death. Miriam had loved to entertain the locals, and was the social leader of the successful farming families, which was less important to Paul, who worked all the time. They had bought some handsome art, which Alex enjoyed although she never used the room and didn't entertain when she was there, and if she did, she did it in the cozy kitchen. There was a formal dining room, which Alex never used either, but her grandparents had. The master suite was upstairs, with two master bedrooms that shared a sitting room. Her grandparents had slept in separate bedrooms, as most people of their generation did. There was a little den on their floor, which had been Miriam's haunt and favorite place for tea with her women friends.

On the third floor was Victoria's old childhood bedroom, where Alex stayed, and her playroom, plus two guest rooms, with an entire warren of small bedrooms on the top floor for the servants. None of them lived in anymore, and came by the day since her grandfather's death. These were modern times, and the employees preferred to live in their own homes, work by day, and then leave. It allowed them to have families and lives that old-time servants didn't. Not living there herself full-time, Alex didn't expect them to live in, as long as the house was cared for properly. Oliver noticed that it was impeccable, and everything in it was of the finest quality. Miriam had loved exceptional furniture and beautiful art, none of which interested her daughter when she left for Europe, stayed in France, and never came back.

Alex loved living in her mother's childhood room on the third floor, when she stayed there. It was large and sunny, decorated in pink silks from France that were rarely seen in farm country, but Miriam Peterson had collected beautiful things and her husband had indulged her. Victoria's childhood bedroom, although less grand than Miriam's room, which Alex felt was a little too fancy and grown-up for her, was lovely. She preferred Victoria's girlhood room, which was grand enough. She had picked her grandfather's room for Oliver to stay in. It was full of beautiful books, and handsome bronze sculptures of western life by Frederic Remington. Alex's grandfather had had many of them, and with Remington's death eleven years before, his collection had become extremely valuable. Alex thought Oliver would enjoy them, so had opened her grandfather's bedroom for him to stay in, which was a treat, and he admired it when he saw it.

Discovering Alex's universe in Beardstown gave Oliver a whole new view of her than the little he had seen in New York. She had thrived in her Illinois life since she had come to the States three years before. She had integrated her American grandfather's world and culture with her European background, and the culture she had grown up with in France. It made her all the more interesting, and made Oliver love her all the more when he saw her in her home, and not merely as a young summer intern in New York. At a young age, she was already a woman of many cultures. He knew she would have a wealth of subjects to write about one day, when she would feel ready to write a book. It fascinated him that she appeared to be American, and even sounded like it at times, but wasn't. She was just subtly different, but it made her much more exciting than all the women he'd ever met.

As Alex preferred, they had dinner in the kitchen that night. Alice, the housekeeper, had set the table for them with Miriam's linens and they ate the delicious stew and a cake Alice had made from a Viennese recipe that Paul had loved, a rich chocolate Sacher torte with raspberry filling, served with whipped cream. Oliver loved it. Alex readily admitted that she didn't know how to cook, and had no interest in it.

"You have other talents," he said and kissed her.

They retired to their bedrooms early that night. Oliver was tired after the long drive, although he enjoyed the evening with her, and he was touched to be put in her grandfather's bedroom, and felt like the honored guest he was.

The next day, Alex took Oliver to the newspaper after breakfast, and introduced him to Josiah Webster. Josiah showed them around, and pointed out to Oliver all the technical details that fascinated him. The paper was state-of-the-art in all its equipment, which had been her grandfather's passion, the modernization of everything. It put other bigger papers to shame with the equipment they had. She and Oliver talked about it animatedly over lunch, and Oliver was excited by what he'd seen.

"You're going to love running this place one day," he said enthusiastically, but she was still hesitant.

"My grandfather was such a big person, it makes me feel very small."

"But you're not small, Alex. You're huge, and with your talent for writing, you could take your grandfather's paper to the next level. It's one of the best small newspapers in the country and can compete with the best of them." Newspapers were a man's world and Alex was afraid to leap in and drown. Even writing a book seemed less daunting. "With the management your grandfather left you, you could do it. I know you can. I can help you." And then he realized what he'd said and what it meant. Helping her meant he would have to stick around to do so, and they had carefully avoided talking about the future, and lived entirely in the present. She wasn't even twenty-one yet and hadn't finished college. Her age was one of the things that made him hesitate. She was so young, and what did he have to offer her? He was just a reporter, no matter how good he was at his job. And soon he would be a published author, which seemed like a more important step than his career in journalism. He didn't want to be a crime reporter forever. Alex wanted to be part of both worlds too, but it scared her when she thought about it. She knew she wasn't ready to run the newspaper, and she didn't want to ruin what her grandfather had so carefully created.

She took Oliver to see some of the neighboring farms, and he thought the area was beautiful, and some of it reminded him of Pennsylvania where he grew up, although he had lived in the city. He marveled at how lucky Alex had been to land there during the war, but she had been so much less fortunate, losing everyone she had loved, and ending up alone at such a young age. He admired her courage and fortitude even more than her beauty, and was touched by how shy she was, with other people. But she was comfortable with him.

They went to church together on Christmas Eve, and ate dinner in the dining room afterward. The housekeeper had prepared a goose for them, which was delicious, and Alex cooked a turkey herself, with Oliver's help, on Christmas Day. They both agreed it was the nicest Christmas they'd ever had.

"My mother always tried to acknowledge Thanksgiving, even though it's not a holiday in France, she wanted me to experience it. But it was a workday for them, and she wasn't much of a cook, so we'd wind up eating at ten o'clock at night, and sometimes the turkey wasn't totally cooked, so we'd eat sausages instead." Alex laughed at the memory she shared with him, and Oliver looked wistful.

"We stopped celebrating holidays after my father left. My mother was too depressed, and I've hated holidays ever since." But Alex had changed that. She improved everything. They joined some people from the church to go caroling on Christmas Day, and it was fun. Some children joined them, and Oliver had a deep voice, and the carolers came to the house for cider afterward. Oliver chatted with them and enjoyed it.

"It must be beautiful here in summer," Oliver said to her after they left, and she nodded and said it was. "This would be a wonderful place to write."

"It is," but she'd been in New York for the past two summers, so she hadn't spent much time in Beardstown. "Maybe you can come out this summer—the Fourth of July is a big deal here, with lots of picnics and a parade down Main Street. There are still some Civil War vets who walk in it with all their medals." She smiled at the thought.

Oliver left on New Year's Day, with great regret because of leaving her, and because he'd had the best holiday of his life.

She was sad to see him go, and they had shared a nostalgic New Year's Eve the night before. At breakfast on New Year's Day, she turned to him.

"When will I see you again, Ollie?" It was the question he always ran from, but she braved it.

"I don't know," he said honestly. Not knowing had kept her from doing anything foolish with him while he was there. There was always something fragile and uncertain between them, because of his fear of commitment. Their relationship was wonderful, but always seemed fleeting and tenuous. "I won't have any vacation for a while," he answered, dodging the question. She nodded, knowing she had none from school in the accelerated program, except for a few days here and there.

Alex was going back to Chicago herself in two days, to start classes again. It had been a wonderful interlude with Oliver during the holidays. He had managed to squeeze ten days out of the newspaper, with some extra days traded with other reporters in order to spend them with her. He had to make up for it now. The passion between them had made it hard to resist the temptation to go too far sometimes, but she didn't want to do anything that neither was ready for. It would ruin everything if she got pregnant, so they had been strong in their resolve, although they could easily have given in to temptation, but he respected her too much to do so.

There were tears in her eyes when she kissed him for the last time and he got into the truck with Horace for the drive to Chicago to catch the train to New York.

"Write to me," Alex said when he rolled down the window.

"I'll try," he said, but he readily acknowledged that it wasn't his forte. He hated writing to anybody, even to her, and she knew he loved her, more than ever now. She would just have to keep busy at school, and hope he'd come to see her again when he could. She was thinking of applying for a real job at the paper in

New York for after she graduated in September, but she wasn't sure.

She waved as they drove away, and walked back into the house. She and Oliver had been happy there together for ten days, and he loved the *Courier*. All the ingredients were there for a good life together, but she had no idea, given their respective wounds and scars from the past, if it would ever happen. There was no way of knowing with Oliver if he would retreat, bolt and run, or seize the future with both hands. Alex knew she had to make her decisions for herself. And as much as she loved him, she couldn't depend on Oliver.

Chapter 15

In the four months after his Christmas visit, Oliver wrote to Alex more regularly, but he made no mention of coming to see her again, and she didn't press him. They were both busy, he was finishing his book, and she was buried in her final year of studies to earn her diploma. And she had no idea when she would see Oliver again.

Alex had classes all day in Chicago on her birthday. It was another holiday she chose to ignore now every year, since there was no one to celebrate it with her. She didn't tell her classmates what day it was. She wasn't close to them. She studied too hard to have a social life. She took two books out of the library for her literature class, and went back to her room at the dorm to study. It was a blustery spring day, as it was every year, and sometimes it snowed in Chicago in April.

The dorm supervisor at the desk glanced at her when she walked in with her blond hair flying. "You have a visitor," she said. "He's been waiting for two hours in the drawing room." Alex couldn't imagine who it was, and walked in. She thought it might be her grandfather's attorney. He had some papers she had to sign for the estate, for her inheritance. It was her twenty-first birthday. She walked in expecting to see him, and Oliver, a huge bouquet of roses on the chair next to him, uncurled his long legs and stood up, and Alex was stunned to see him.

"Oh my God! What are you doing here?"

"I know someone in Chicago having a birthday, so I came for the night." He glanced at the chair next to him. "The roses are for her, but you can have them if you want," he said, putting the flowers in her arms and giving her a quick kiss, before anyone could see them. Public displays of affection with male visitors were strictly forbidden. "Can I interest you in dinner?"

"Yes!" she said with delight, and snuck another kiss. "Where are we going, what'll I wear?" She was thrilled that Oliver had remembered the date and come.

"Whatever you want. Today is your day."

"You came all the way from New York for my birthday?" she said in disbelief, and he grinned, pleased with her response.

"I owe you a letter, and I'd rather come to see you than send you another postcard. Besides, I missed you." He had written to her, but not frequently, and he had started a second book, another crime novel. He had found his niche. The first one hadn't sold yet, but his agent felt sure it would soon, and Oliver was hopeful, and already engrossed in his new book.

Alex took the roses to her room with her, put them in a vase on her dresser, and was back twenty minutes later, dressed for dinner. They had dinner at the restaurant of his hotel, and caught up on all the news since Christmas. She told him she didn't have a job yet for the fall, but she had written to the *World,* and they hadn't responded yet. She had asked if there was any department more mainstream and interesting than the society column at the paper. But Oliver had told her that as a woman, they were unlikely to hire her for any other section, except for the general secretarial pool and she had better skills than that, after college. She didn't really care, as long as she found a job and could be near him. It was hard being so far away from each other all the time, and it was wearing on both of them. She had another four and a half months at the University of Chicago before she got her diploma. They were in the home stretch, but it seemed long to her.

The evening rushed past them like an express train, but she was touched that he had made so much effort to be with her on her birthday. He was always attentive and thoughtful and loving, except when he was deeply immersed in writing, or in one of his dark moods, which still happened from time to time. She was getting used to it, and recognized the signs when he became unresponsive. But he bounced back now faster than he used to, usually in a week or two.

He took a midnight train back to New York and wouldn't let her come to the station with him. He said it would be too dangerous at that hour for her to go back to the dorm alone.

She hadn't seen him in four months and savored every moment with him. They were becoming experts at enduring a long-distance relationship, despite his erratic communication skills, which were still spotty. But he had won major points for the birthday visit, and he had given her a little silver charm bracelet with a silver heart on it, with the date, which was thoughtful. He had given her a book of poetry too.

Oliver's fellow reporters in the Crime pool were surprised that he and Alex were still hanging in after two years, and told him it was the price to pay for being in love with a schoolgirl, and not an adult, waiting for her to grow up, but Oliver seemed happy.

He came to Beardstown three months later for the Fourth of July, and it was just as festive and picturesque as Alex had promised. He loved the area as much in the summer as he did in winter. He and Josiah were happy to see each other and chatted at length about some new printing machines they had acquired that were twice as fast as the old ones, and the paper in New York didn't have them yet. Paul had never minded spending money on state-of-the-art equipment which increased efficiency, so Josiah was operating along the same lines. Oliver was able to spend four days with her over the holiday, with some careful trading with his colleagues.

The paper had written to her four weeks earlier and offered her a job in Society. In addition to her normal duties, she was going to write the copy for all three branches of the department. Sylvia Bates was delighted that she was coming back, to stay this time. She had written Alex a personal note and said that she hoped they'd be celebrating her twenty-fifth anniversary at the paper one day, like Sylvia. None of them knew that she owned a newspaper in the Midwest. Only Oliver knew, and he was discreet about it. But it gave her options for the future that the others didn't have. They had offered her a very decent salary, for a woman. But it still didn't compare to what the male reporters were paid, although her work wouldn't be as dangerous as Oliver's, which made a difference. She wouldn't be covering members of the mob, or reporting on crime scenes littered with bodies. She would be attending weddings and debutante balls, and social events that involved stage and screen stars and celebrities, and she needed the wardrobe to go with it.

Oliver was thrilled she was coming back, and he promised to help her find an apartment, hopefully close to his. They were both excited about her return to New York City, after twelve long months apart by the time she got there.

He came out for her graduation in September, which was small, since the main ceremony was normally in May, but there was a small ceremony for the dedicated students in her program. She was the only woman, and all of the others were married and some had children, which was their reason for wanting to get their diplomas sooner, to help them get better jobs to support their wives and children. Alex wanted hers so she could join the workforce and get a real job in New York, and be near Oliver, and she was tired of school by then.

She arrived in New York a week after she got her diploma, and reported for work on the Monday following her arrival. She had found an apartment that weekend. It was a small studio, in a brownstone within walking distance of Oliver. It was tiny compared to her room in the dorm, and smaller than her dressing room in her grandfather's home, but it was her first apartment. It was furnished, so all she had to do was unpack when she got there. The furniture wasn't beautiful, and it was old, but it was clean and the one room she had was sunny. It came with linens and kitchen equipment, and she didn't need anything more. Alex wasn't spoiled or extravagant, and adapted to whatever she had. She didn't want to spend a fortune on rent, and was trying to live on her salary, although she didn't have to. And having seen her home, Oliver admired her for being so restrained. She wasn't a frivolous person.

Some of the faces had changed at Society when she showed up for work. Melanie was gone, but the three editors were still there. There were some new girls who seemed nice. All of them were older than Alex. She was always the youngest person in the room, but didn't mind it, and she got along with her coworkers. Sylvia considered herself her mentor, and had recommended her for the job, for which Alex was grateful.

On the day she arrived, Alex and Oliver began their regular lunches again, and Sylvia kept asking her when she thought they'd get engaged.

"Maybe never," Alex said honestly. It had been two years and there was no sign of it. They were comfortable as they were. "We both want careers, and marriage isn't compatible with that, not for women anyway."

"Maybe you should start dating other men," Sylvia said pensively, "to make him jealous." She'd never been married, since her long-term lover already was, and he was Catholic and would never leave his wife. But she loved giving everyone advice. Alex had no desire to meet or date other men—she liked the one she had. She had read in the paper that Phillip Baxter had gotten engaged and was getting married in the fall. His fiancée had come out at the New York deb ball two years before, and was a year younger than Alex. Alex had liked him when they met, but their daily lives were just too far apart with him at Yale, and her in Chicago, and once she met Oliver, Phillip just seemed like a nice boy to her. By normal standards, Alex should have been married by then, or at least engaged. But she had no desire to give up her independence. Sylvia told her to watch out for that, that it was dangerous and could become a habit, and make Alex unsuitable for any man. And at thirty-eight, Oliver was slipping into the category of confirmed bachelor.

They cooked a turkey together in his apartment for Thanksgiving and a week later, he was excited when he met her for lunch in the cafeteria. He whispered the news to her, so no one would hear him. "My agent has a publisher for my book." His eyes were alight with excitement and she was thrilled for him. His dream was coming true. "They're offering me a three-book contract for the first one, the one I'm working on now, and the next one." He already had an outline for it. He was on his way.

"That's fantastic!" she whispered back. "I'm so proud of you!" He was beaming.

"I think I'll quit on the first of the year. I can coast for quite a while now." They were paying him handsomely for the three-book contract, and she knew he had money saved. He'd been hoping for something like that. "And it's a good publisher." He was ecstatic.

"Can't you wait for a while to quit?" she said in a whisper. "I just got here." She'd only been there for two months in her new job.

"I'm dying to get out of here. If I see one more crime scene, I think I may kill someone myself. I've had enough." She knew it was true, although her job would be much less fun if he wasn't there. But she knew she didn't have a right to impact his career just so she would have someone to have lunch with. It wouldn't be fair to him. "Let's celebrate this weekend," he said. "I'm off." Every weekend he didn't work felt like a vacation to them. She patted his hand and smiled, profoundly happy for him. And his books were great. He deserved a lucky break. She brought a bottle of champagne home for him that night, and he had made a reservation at Delmonico's for Saturday night, his favorite fancy restaurant, and she was looking forward to it too. They were in a very adult relationship for a girl her age, and it was getting harder and harder to keep it chaste, ever since she'd been back in New York and they saw each other every day. It was particularly hard when he came to her apartment, since almost the entire apartment was taken up by the bed, and there was no couch, just two straight-backed chairs at a drop-leaf dining table, so if they wanted to sit anywhere more comfortable, they wound up on her bed and went further than they intended. She didn't know how much longer she could hold out. They wanted each other so badly, but were still trying to resist. And given the risk, she didn't want to cross that line yet. Neither of them wanted to get married just so they could have sex.

* * *

They were both disappointed when his weekend off got canceled on Friday. The paper had been tipped off about a big meeting between the Lucchese, Gambino, and Genovese families over the massively lucrative illegal alcohol sales in New York. Tommy was going to cover it, but got sick, and Oliver was assigned to it instead. So Alex and Oliver had to postpone their dinner at Delmonico's to celebrate his book contract. They put it off to the following week.

The meeting was scheduled downtown in the meatpacking district at a warehouse that the Luccheses owned, and all three big Mafia bosses were going to be there to parcel out the districts. If the meeting went well, it was going to be profitable for all three families. If it didn't, it would be a bloodbath that could start a war. Oliver didn't discuss it with Alex, not wanting to worry her, but she could tell that he was distracted and tense when he left for work on Saturday after he met her for lunch. He had hardly listened to a word she said, and he had told her on Friday that he was meeting with some informants who had information for him. She could understand why he wanted to quit. All his time was spent reporting on dead bodies and dealing with the lowest criminal element in the world. And the police were almost as corrupt as the mob, and were hand in glove with them. There were constant scandals about cops on the take. It was the seamy side of life, while she wrote about society weddings in glowing terms. Sometimes she and Oliver laughed about the extreme opposites they dealt with in their jobs.

Alex had errands to do on Saturday, and used the time to do menial chores she didn't have time to take care of during the week. When Oliver was working, she could do the things that bored him, like buy stockings she needed for work, go to the dry cleaner, return library books, and get her hair done. It was a blessing sometimes when he was busy. Although this time she had an uneasy feeling about what he was doing. He had been so distracted and preoccupied that she had a feeling it was something big. He hadn't said a word about it to her. He never did when it came to stories about the mob families—he kept them to himself. He didn't want her to worry.

He had told her that his assignment would go late that night and he wouldn't see her, which wasn't unusual, but something didn't feel right and kept gnawing at her. She finally realized what it was as she lay in her bed that night trying to read. It occurred to her that he had looked scared, which was something he never did. Oliver was never physically afraid. It worried her at times, because given some of the assignments he went on, he should have been. He was fearless, and he occasionally misjudged it, like the night he had taken her on assignment with him, and shouldn't have, and a last shooter had come out of the warehouse with guns blazing and they were nearly shot. She had a feeling that he was on that kind of assignment that night, but there was no way to know, or to reach him. She tried calling him at work from a public phone booth, since she didn't have a phone, but the reporter who answered said he wasn't there and he was working in the field. She didn't know the reporter, and he didn't seem to know anything about Oliver's whereabouts. It was obviously a secret operation of some kind. She tried to put her fears out of her mind, and finally went to sleep.

He had told her he would pick her up for lunch the next day if he was free, but he didn't show. She waited around until three o'clock, and tried calling the office again. The reporter who answered fobbed her off, and she decided to do something she'd never done before, go alone to his apartment. Maybe he'd been up all night and was asleep. She had his keys, for an emergency, and decided to use them.

She took a cab to his apartment, let herself in the outer door of the building, and raced up the stairs. She called out when she walked in, not wanting to startle him. He wasn't there. She looked around, and he hadn't slept in his bed. It was possible that he was somewhere on a concealed mission, hoping for a break, sleeping in a car while they waited. Anything was possible. Or at the other end of the spectrum, he could be injured or dead, although that was unlikely. But she felt panic rising in her throat. She hadn't eaten all day, and she waited a little longer. She was starving and decided to go down the street and get something to eat while she waited for him. There were two lemons and a beer in his fridge. She wasn't going to leave until he came home.

She put on her coat and walked to the deli, bought a turkey sandwich, and walked past a newsstand on the way back. Her eyes stopped on the front page of the afternoon edition of the *World*. The headline read "Carnage on Tenth Avenue." It had happened in the meatpacking district again, which was where the mob families were trafficking a lot of the alcohol they were selling. Alex walked straight to the newsstand, picked up a copy of the paper, and looked at the details. It said accurately that three of the most important mob families had had a summit meeting in the early hours of the morning on Saturday to redistribute the territories of illegal alcohol sales, and the meeting had erupted in violence. The theory was touched on in the newspaper article that there had been foul play before the meeting and it had been an ambush. Seven of the twenty-nine "family" members at the meeting had been shot and killed at the scene, five had been severely wounded, three more had died in ambulances on the way to the hospital, four bystand-ers had been critically injured, and two policemen were dead. In all, twelve people were dead, and nine critically injured. It was the worst clash of its kind between warring Mafia families that had been seen in many, many years. Alex knew instantly as she read it that Oliver was there. He had to be, it was why he had seemed so nervous, and she was terrified that he was one of the critically injured bystanders. She just hoped he wasn't dead. They hadn't released the names of the victims. She ran to a pay phone and called the Crime desk, and asked again if they knew Oliver's whereabouts. The voice on the phone asked someone next to them and the answer was negative. "This is Oliver Foster's girlfriend," she said without hesitation. "Do you know where they took the injured victims from the massacre yesterday?" The reporter on the phone asked the one next to him, and responded, "Lenox Hill Hospital." She called the oper-ator then, and asked to be connected to the hospital. Someone answered after several long rings, and she asked if Oliver Foster had been admitted. The wait was interminable again, and they connected her to the E.R. and she asked the same question. The nurse went to check the patient roster and came back on the line with an ice-cold voice.

"I'm sorry I cannot give you that information," and there was a click in Alex's ear and the line went dead. She suspected that the warring families were liable to come back and finish the job on the victims, and the hospital was trying to avoid it. There was no other choice but to go there. If she hadn't called the newspaper, she'd have been waiting all day. She hailed a cab and gave the driver the address.

"Are you okay?" he asked her, with a glance in the rearview mirror. She was young and pretty, and she didn't look sick. She wasn't likely to cause a problem in his cab. He didn't want any trouble. He had read about the Mafia war too.

When they got to the hospital, she gave him a twenty-dollar bill, five times the amount on the meter, and leapt out to find Oliver somewhere in the bowels of the hospital. She had a terrible feeling that he was there and needed her. She ran from one department to the next while they gave her the runaround, and insisted he wasn't there, and then she saw a lineup of familiar faces in a surgical waiting room. They were all from the Crime room, and she approached them discreetly, lowering her voice to barely more than a whisper.

"Do any of you know if Oliver Foster is on the list of injured victims?" Two shook their heads and the others denied it. "Please tell me the truth," she said, begging them. "I'm Alex Bouvier, from Society, I work there." She looked young and innocent and distraught, and one of the young reporters spoke up.

"He's here," the younger man said. He pointed to the nursing desk. "Ask her, she'll tell you where he is." Alex went to the desk then to speak to the nurse. Clearly something had happened. That much wasn't a secret. The rest was, including the names of the victims. She asked for Oliver again, and the nurse hesitated and consulted her patient list. There were strict rules being applied to the wounded, and Alex noticed then that there were police and hospital security lining the halls. Clearly, they were afraid of reprisals, and the murder of innocent victims who had nothing to do with it. The nurse asked Alex for her relationship to the patient, and she combed her mind for a minute to find the right lie to convince the nurse to let her see him. She considered sister, but didn't think it was strong enough, mother wasn't credible, wife was ridiculous, and she looked too old to be his daughter. She finally went with daughter and hoped the nurse believed her. The nurse looked at her closely and doubted it, but she didn't say a word and pointed to the right cubicle. Alex looked so distraught she didn't want to deny her access, on the off chance that what she said was true.

Alex squeezed in between two mint-colored curtains hung from a rod above the bed, and she wouldn't have recognized Oliver if the nurse hadn't directed her. He had been intubated and was unconscious. He had a huge bandage on his chest, and another one on his upper thigh, and a young doctor was checking his pulse.

"How is he?" The young resident turned around when she spoke, startled. He hadn't heard her come in, and they were on high alert for a potential shootout in the hospital, which would terrorize the other patients and visitors.

"He's hanging on. Did they clear you at the desk? Only the next of kin are being admitted."

"I'm his daughter." She prayed that no one would ask to see proof, or her ID with a different name.

"He took a bullet," the doctor explained in a soft voice. "Two, in fact—one was a direct hit, the other ricocheted and exited. The hit nicked his lung, the ricochet went through his upper thigh and exited." Both wound sites sounded painful. "Your dad's a reporter?" She nodded and at least that was true. "You probably shouldn't be in here, but I'll let you stay for a little while. He just came out of recovery, after the surgery. We'll bring him back to consciousness tomorrow if his vitals are strong. He's doing better now. They saved him in the ambulance before we got him." It was upsetting the way they talked about him, like a thing or an object. Alex was praying he'd survive, by some miracle. None of it sounded good to her. He looked terrible.

"What's the prognosis?"

"If he makes it through tonight, he should make it. If they don't shoot him again. We're on high alert for that." He left then and a nurse took his place and checked Oliver's dressings and vital signs. Alex was deathly pale, and took up as little space as she could, until a nurse asked her to step outside. She was going to check the bandage on his thigh. Alex went outside and slid into a chair in the waiting area. She didn't go back in for an hour. She felt too weak to stand up again and thought she might faint, and then she asked at the desk how he was doing. "He's stable," was all they told her.

Half an hour later she went back in. Nothing had changed,

and she sat down in a small straight-backed chair in the room and didn't move all night. The nurses seemed to have forgotten her when they came to do their checks. It was all very brisk and mechanical. They checked him all night, and in the morning a doctor stepped in and noticed Alex and asked her to step outside. When she went back in after he'd left, the breathing tube was gone, which she thought was a good sign. There had been constant activity in the ward all night. Oliver was fighting for his life. She sat down in the chair again, and a young nurse asked her if she needed anything. Alex thanked her and shook her head. She went to get a cup of coffee from a pot the nurses had brewing in their staff room. She took a drink of water from the fountain, and continued her vigil. What seemed like hours later, Tommy stuck his head in Oliver's cubicle and saw her. He looked surprised. He walked over and whispered to her.

"How is he?"

"I don't know. He's been unconscious since I got here yesterday." Tommy nodded and left after a few minutes, and Alex met him in the hallway two hours later. He looked exhausted.

"Any news?" Tommy asked her.

"No change."

"They killed one of our guys, the photographer. The whole thing was awful. You look terrible. Have you eaten?" he said bluntly, and she shook her head. He brought her a sandwich from the cafeteria a little while later, and she thanked him and ate it, and felt better. A nurse and a doctor were with Oliver when she went back to him. An alarm was sounding on one of the monitors and they were watching him closely. She spent the second night on the chair in his cubicle, and in the morning, he moaned and moved a little, and then he opened his eyes and saw Alex. His voice was a croak when he whispered to her. "Why are you here?"

"Because I love you," she whispered back. He smiled and closed his eyes and squeezed her hand, and went back to sleep. When the nurse returned, Alex told her.

She smiled at Alex. "He's better. His vital signs are stronger." Alex went home to shower and change then. It was Tuesday. She slept for an hour and went back, and Oliver opened his eyes again and saw her when she walked in and stood next to him.

"How do you feel?" she asked him.

"Tired. You should go home," he whispered and drifted back to sleep. He hovered between life and death for a week, and then he was more alert, and they moved him to a less acute area of the emergency unit. The papers were full of the mob shooting, and Tommy visited him several times. Alex was beginning to breathe again, when they moved him. It had been a terrifying ten days. Another member of one of the families had been assassinated in his home as revenge.

"Your dad's feeling better," one of the nurses said, smiling at Alex encouragingly, and Oliver looked at Alex with a question when the nurse left the room.

"What did she say?" He looked puzzled.

"I told her you were my father so they let me in. Only next of kin could see you, so I lied," she said, and he grimaced.

"I guess I deserve that, with someone your age. You look exhausted." He squeezed her hand.

"Thanks, you too." She smiled at him. It was good to hear him talk and stay awake for more than five minutes.

It took another week for him to sit up in bed. Alex slept at home in her own bed that night, and woke up nine hours later and rushed back to the hospital. There was a police officer outside Oliver's door when she got there.

"What happened? Why the palace guard?" she asked Oliver.

"Apparently, the Luccheses want to know who set them up. They want to make sure it wasn't us. They're livid. At everybody."

"Yeah. I'm livid too. It's shocking to go around shooting the press. Not to mention killing them. I hope you get combat pay for this." She was upset, and he shook his head.

"No, just sick leave. I'm off for a month, more if I need it. The doctor said I can go home in a couple of weeks."

"Maybe you'd be safer there." She was worried about him.

"I'm okay, Alex, I promise. I'm sorry I put you through this."

"I'm sorry they put you through this. They're savages. I hope you do quit after this, or transfer to a more civilized department."

"They pay us better in Crime."

"Now you know why." He'd been reading the paper when she walked in. Tommy had brought it. More of the victims had died, one of them a cop. The three families were on a rampage, and the city was in an uproar. One of the informants had been killed. It was a gang war of major proportions. "Will they come after you when you go home?"

"I don't think so. They know who their enemies are. Usually, they like us."

"It's a hell of a way to treat people they like."

"It was an accident. They were shooting each other and I got in the way." Alex had taken an unpaid leave from work to be with him, and had missed a big deb ball she was supposed to cover. Christmas had sailed past them while he was unconscious and Alex didn't care. She just wanted him to live and be all right. But he was out of danger now. A few days later they had him walk down the hall with a nurse on one side and Alex on the other, and the police officer assigned to protect him right behind him. The other victims had police guards too. And all of the members of the mob families had been removed to a hospital on Long Island that they owned. No one had been charged yet because no one was talking, and probably never would. No one would risk it. Alex looked at Oliver seriously when he got back to bed.

"You have to quit, Ollie, this is too dangerous," and it was her worst nightmare, losing him.

"I will quit. Not yet. The paper is paying all of my medical bills."

"I don't want to lose you."

"It won't happen again," he reassured her.

"It will. Whatever the paper pays you, it's not worth it. I want to go home to Beardstown and take you with me."

"We'll do that. Just not yet."

A week later, almost at the end of January, they let him go home. Alex had missed all the holiday events that were part of her job, but Sylvia knew why and wasn't complaining. She told Alex to take all the time she needed. They were all grateful that Oliver was alive.

When they let him go home, Alex went with him to take care of him. She was a wonderful nurse and even cooked for him. She took care of him like a child. He was watching her bustle around his bedroom one day, as she made the bed and fluffed his pillows for him and helped him into bed. His wounds were healing well, but he had lost a lot of blood and was still weak.

"You're amazing," he told her, and pulled her onto the bed next to him, and kissed her, and all the terror they had lived through was swept away on a wave of passion, as though they had to prove to themselves that they were still alive and death couldn't claim him. They had held back for so long, and could no longer control it. The dam had broken and all their fears and love for each other were laid bare. They were careful with his leg and they were both breathless when it was over. Oliver lay there for a moment not moving, with his eyes closed, breathing heavily, and she panicked.

"Are you okay? Did I hurt you?" There was blood on the bed because it was her first time, and he opened his eyes and looked at her with everything he felt for her. "I love you so much it hurts," he whispered and kissed her. She felt the same way. She thought she would die if he did. She couldn't bear losing him too. She lay in bed with him, her clothes on the floor with his pajamas, and he admired her perfectly sculpted body. She knew she belonged to him at that moment.

They made love again that night and in the morning. All their caution and restraint for so long, almost three years, was forgotten. They needed each other desperately, like two starving people. His near death had rattled both of them.

They went for a walk in his neighborhood that afternoon and he saw how frightened she was. She was terrified the mobsters would come back and kill him, but it was a quiet Sunday afternoon, and no one approached them.

"The managing editor spoke to the families this week," he told her. "They apologized for what happened to us. They gave a very big bequest to the photographer's widow."

"And what about you?" she asked him with a cynical look.

"They said they were sorry. It was an accident."

"They're animals. They all belong in prison."

"That's true. But they own this city and Chicago, half the businesses, and most of the cops. This is their world right now. Prohibition has put them where they've wanted to be for a long time, in the driver's seat."

"And they ran over you, Ollie. You could have died. I would have died, if you did."

"I know, baby. I'm meeting with the managing editor tomorrow. I'm going to quit." She looked relieved when he said it, as though a thousand-pound weight had been taken off her back.

He looked handsome and healthy when he left for his meeting the next day. She left when he did, to go to her apartment and take care of some things. She had done nothing but care for him for the past six weeks. She was still on unpaid leave from her job. She wanted to put some order back in her life, and after he quit, they could figure out the future. She had taken a big step, a giant leap of faith when she made love with him. Her life and her future were on the line now. She had cast her lot with his, with total faith in him. And if she got pregnant, she knew they'd face it together. He had protected her after the first time, but she might have gotten pregnant and they both knew it. It was a huge step for her, for them both. She had no regrets, and he said he had none either. They belonged to each other.

She went back to his apartment late that afternoon. He was drinking a scotch, which he said eased the pain when he had any. But he had healed well. She smiled as soon as she saw him.

"What did the editor say when you told him?" she asked, and sat down on the couch next to him with a smile.

Oliver was silent for a moment and she looked at him, as though she didn't understand. Something was wrong. He didn't answer her. He had had the scotch to give himself courage. "You quit, right?"

"They made me head of Crime. To compensate me for the accident."

"That wasn't an 'accident,' Ollie. It was a gunfight between gangsters and they didn't care if they killed you, and neither did the goddam paper. It's not your job to die for them, or is it? They gave you a big promotion so you'd be a good sport about being shot for them. This isn't the army, you're not fighting for your country. It's a gang war, and you don't matter to them. You matter to me. I love you. They don't." She was crying when she said it.

"It's a huge promotion, Alex, and a lot of prestige with it. I'll never be out in the field like that again. If I do it for a couple of years, and write the books, I'll have something solid to offer you, to bring to the table when I marry you."

"You can't marry me if you're dead," she said angrily. She couldn't take it anymore. "And what if I got pregnant, if our baby had no father, or you get killed next year or the year after. I can't tell you what to do, that's up to you. This is just another excuse for you not to make a commitment. You'd rather get shot than do that. Well, I think what you're doing is a hell of a lot scarier. And all I can tell you is what I'm going to do. I'm going home, to Beardstown, to my home, and the newspaper my grandfather was so proud of. I'm going to work there every morning and try to learn the business. And then I'm going to write for the rest of the day. I want to write a book, that's my dream, *and* run the paper. If you want to come with me, we can run the paper together, whether you marry me or not. And you can write your books, and we can have a real live newspaper we're proud of, together, and we can both write our books. And if we have a child or children one day, we can give them a good life. But I'm not going to stay here and write about parties I don't care about, for a paper that doesn't care about either of us, until you turn into some bitter, cynical old man who missed the boat on life. And you'll be dead by then, if they kill you. I'm not going to miss that boat, for you, or anyone else. I'm going home. If you want to come with me, great, that's what I can offer you, a good life, a real life, to share what I have with you. If that's not what you want, then good luck. I hope you don't get shot again. Next time you might not be as lucky. Next time maybe they'll shoot you in the back instead of the chest, like the rest of their victims they find in the river tied to a block of cement. I'm leaving tomorrow. See you on the train, or not. It's up to you."

He was so shocked by the force of what she'd said that he was speechless for a moment. She stood, picked up her purse, and walked out of his apartment before he could stop her or even speak. He felt paralyzed and didn't know what to do. The job they had offered him was nearly irresistible, at three times his current salary, except that he'd had to get shot and nearly die to get it. He sat there staring into space in the silent apartment after she left. He was thinking of what she'd said. He knew she was right but he didn't know if he was ready. She was braver and stronger than he was and she wasn't even twenty-two yet. She was the strongest woman he'd ever known, and he loved her, but he didn't know if he had the guts to do what she wanted. If not, she had made herself clear. She was leaving for Chicago and going home, with or without him.

Chapter 16

Alex went to see Sylvia at the paper the next morning. She wore a simple black suit and her blond hair was pulled back. She looked serious when she walked into Sylvia's office and asked if she had a minute. Sylvia was happy to see her and invited her in to sit down.

"How's Oliver?" she asked kindly. "He scared the hell out of all of us. Thank God he survived. That was an awful business." Alex didn't say anything. She agreed, but it happened every day, and would again. It was how those "families" worked and how they did business, no matter how many lives it cost. It was just business to them.

"I wanted to give you this personally," Alex said quietly, and handed Sylvia a letter across her desk. "It's my letter of resignation. I loved working for you, and you were wonderful to me, but I'm going home."

"To Chicago?" Sylvia could see what it was immediately, and had guessed from the look on Alex's face.

"To Beardstown, Illinois." Alex smiled. "It's a tiny town in farm country. I have an opportunity at a paper there, in management."

"That doesn't sound like the job for you, Alex," Sylvia said seriously.

"I think it is. Or it will be. And there are some other things I want to do. I want to write, and that's hard to do here in New York. There are a lot of distractions."

"Like boyfriends who get shot," Sylvia said with a rueful smile.

"Yeah, like that." Alex smiled back at her. She was subdued, and sad to leave the job. And Sylvia had been kind to her.

"You'll get a lot further here in your career," Sylvia insisted, but she knew she had already lost the argument. She could see that Alex had made up her mind.

"This isn't what I want," Alex said quietly.

"And Oliver?"

"That's up to him. They promoted him to the head of Crime for getting shot. That's a hard way to get a promotion."

"Is he staying?"

"Probably." Alex was realistic. She had thought about it all night and she doubted that Oliver would have the guts to leave New York and a big job for a hick town miles from anything with nothing but cows and corn around, and a small-town newspaper. And it would involve a real commitment to her that she no longer believed he would ever make. She had given up hope when he said he was ready to take the promotion as the head of Crime.

"Maybe he'll surprise you," Sylvia said gently. She doubted it too. "You never know." Alex stood up then and thanked her. Sylvia hugged her and there were tears in both women's eyes. "Stay in touch and call me if you come to New York. I have a feeling that book you want to write will be a knockout." She meant it. Alex was a talented, rare find who would go far.

"I hope so." Alex smiled through her tears, and left the office quickly. She didn't stop to say goodbye to Sam or Tommy, because she didn't want to run into Oliver starting his new job.

She had left her bags with the guard in the lobby and took a cab to Grand Central Terminal to catch her train. There would be no one to pick her up in Chicago the next day, to drive her home. She didn't want to bother Horace. She had arranged for a limo service to pick her up and take her to Beardstown.

She slept on the train. She knew she'd done the right thing, but she was sad anyway. She liked Sylvia a lot. It had been exciting working for a major newspaper. She had learned some things she was taking with her, about newspapers. She wondered if she should start a modified society column in the *Courier* about local social events and the people who gave them. People liked reading about people they knew or wished they were. It gave them something to aspire to, and dream of. The principle was a good one. And she was going to write the women's editorial column she had started before. She had already made a list of topics she wanted to address. It was going to be a women's column, all about the issues that mattered to them. It was time that women had a voice in the farming community too, and everywhere else.

Before the train left New York, she stood on the platform for as long as she could, until the last whistle blew, looking for Oliver running down the platform. He never came. She didn't really expect him to, but a part of her had hoped. She had left her heart with him. She knew he wouldn't come now. He had his own path to follow and she couldn't stop him or change that, any more than he could change hers. She had her own mind, and her own ideas and passions and values, and he had his. And they were no longer the same.

She wondered if she had gotten pregnant when they made love. It was too soon to know. If she had, she would bring up the child alone. Other women had done it, and she knew she could if she had to. She would have loved to share a life and family with Oliver, a family with a mother and father who loved each other as much as her parents had. She wanted to be the kind of mother hers had been, full of courage and bold ideas, willing to risk everything for her beliefs, wanting to make a difference in the world and to others, and to pay the price for it without regret. Her mother had risked her life for her dreams at her husband's side, and Alex wanted to do that too.

The train lulled her to sleep that night, and she woke up early the next morning and was dressed and ready when they glided into La Salle Street Station. All her belongings had fit into two suitcases, and she set them down on the platform until the driver came to meet her, and a porter carried the bags to the car waiting outside for them. She didn't know when she'd leave Beardstown again and come back to Chicago. She was going home, and she wanted to stay there for a while, without going anywhere.

She had work to do. She hoped it would help her forget how much she loved Oliver.

The weather was good, and the drive took less than six hours. She had sent Josiah a telegram to say she was coming home. She didn't explain, but he understood that she was coming home to stay. Something must have happened in New York, but she didn't say what. She was like her grandfather—she kept some things to herself, and she had a mind of her own. He was sure she had a plan and would tell him in time, when he needed to know.

When they arrived, walked into the house and up the stairs to her bedroom, it felt like home. She still expected her grandfather to appear whenever she came back to Beardstown, his presence in the house was so strong. But there were a few things she wanted to change now, to make it her own.

She was at the paper the next morning when Josiah arrived. He was happy to see her. They shared a cup of coffee and he brought her up to date. She went to her grandfather's office, and started working on her column. It was about the value of women in the workplace and the jobs they were better suited to than men. It was sure to cause comment and controversy, which had been an important ingredient in her grandfather's columns too. He said it added spice to the subject, and she thought he was right, about that, and so many things he had taught her. His were big shoes to fill but she felt ready to begin her journey into her future.

She followed the schedule she'd set for herself. She worked at the paper until one o'clock every day, or two on heavy days, and then she went home, helped herself to whatever was in the fridge or a piece of fruit, and headed upstairs to her little sitting room. She had an old typewriter of her grandfather's she had put on the desk. The room had a view of the fields beyond her property and a corner of the orchards and the pond. She sat there as long as she needed to, long past dinnertime sometimes, if she bothered to eat. It was harder than she expected, and slow going on some days. Some days she only wrote one page, and on other days it moved at a good clip. She had only two chapters of her book written so far, but she was determined to finish it, however long it took. She had set goals for herself and she intended to stick to them. She remembered her grandfather's words that she could be whatever she wanted to be. She had said she wanted to be a writer when she was six. And she was sticking to that plan. She wanted to run a newspaper too. She was doing both.

She wanted to go back to France for a visit one day too, but she knew she wasn't ready to do that yet. The memories were still painful. She owned her grandmother's apartment, and the same tenant was in it, four years after she had left. She was turning twenty-two, and the war seemed a long time ago, and the life she had lived there as a child before the war. She still thought of Mamie-Thérèse frequently, and would always miss her.

She knew she wasn't pregnant by then. She had been both relieved and disappointed when she found out she wasn't. It would have been a way of hanging onto part of Oliver, the best part, a product of the love they had shared. And now even that was gone. She hadn't heard from him since she left, and knew she never would. She had to make her peace with it, even though she loved him. Their time was past.

Alex had been in Beardstown for a month, and the fields were turning green. They would turn yellow in summer and the fields would be full of corn. But they were a lush emerald green now. She was on her way from the paper to the house one afternoon, to work on her book, when a car stopped near the house, and a man got out. He had his back to her at first and she didn't recognize him. She wondered if he was lost. No one came all the way down the road to the house unless they were invited, she was expecting them, and she knew who they were. She watched as the stranger turned around, and time stopped for an instant. It was Oliver. They stood looking at each other for an endless moment, like a film that had stopped, and then he walked toward her. She didn't move or smile. She didn't know what to do or say, or what he was doing there. She hadn't heard from him since she walked out of his apartment when he told her about his promotion, and it had been too much for her, after the terror of his being shot.

"Hello, Oliver," were the only words she could muster. "What are you doing here?"

"I was in Chicago on business, and I lost my way and wound up here. Damned if I know how," he said innocently, in his easy way, full of the charm she had tried so hard to forget and almost had. He made her smile.

"Do you want a glass of water before you go back?" she parried, and he laughed.

"That's all I get after a six-hour drive?"

"Maybe so. What did you have in mind? I'm out of scotch and it's against the law here. Prohibition, as you know." It was a sensitive subject for both of them, but they got past the moment.

"I see you've started a women's column in the *Courier.* I like it." She was surprised that he'd seen it.

"How do you know?"

"I had a friend send it to me." She couldn't imagine who. Oliver had written to Josiah to ask how she was and to make sure she was all right, he'd asked Josiah not to tell her, which he had apparently respected, and he'd sent Oliver a copy of the paper. Oliver was impressed—it was so like her, with her clear opinions and bold ideas. He missed her even more when he read it.

Oliver was standing in front of Alex by then, facing her. He was as brave as she was. It had taken courage to come here and he had no idea what she'd say. She might just tell him to get off her property, but he guessed that she was too polite to be that blunt.

"Why did you come here, Ollie?" she asked, looking into his eyes. He looked different, but she wasn't sure why. Maybe he really was in Chicago on business, chasing one of the Gambinos, or a Lucchese, and decided to show up in Beardstown for old times' sake. It was a long way to come just to say hello. "You could have called me at the paper. I have a phone there." She had ordered one for the house too, but she didn't have it yet. She wanted to modernize, just as her grandfather would have.

"I had a job offer here a few months ago, and I wanted to know if it still stands. I quit the morning you left New York. I gave them a month's notice and they gave me a great reference, if you'd like to see it. They gave Tommy the job. He deserves it and he wanted it. So I thought I'd see if the position at the *Courier* is still open—as I recall it was co-publisher, half days, so I could write in the afternoons."

"I started a book," she said, smiling cautiously. She seemed suddenly young again, and not as stern and suspicious as when he'd arrived.

"It's about time," he said, pleased for her. "How's it going?"

"Slowly."

"It'll pick up speed as you go. Do you suppose I could have that glass of water you offered? I'm parched. So is the job still open?"

"I'll have to discuss it with Josiah," she said matter-of-factly, and led the way into the house. He followed her into the familiar kitchen. Josiah had seen the car drive past the newspaper and had guessed who it was. He hoped the meeting turned out well for Alex. He had come to love and respect her while working with her, and he liked Oliver too. He thought they were a good match. And they would make a good team.

Alex handed Oliver the glass of water and didn't invite him to sit down. Their eyes met and held for a moment. "There's something I meant to give you in New York. But things got away from me when I got shot." He reached deep into his pocket and pulled out a small black leather jeweler's box, and held it out to her. She hesitated and didn't take it from him. "It's yours—you can keep it as a souvenir if you want. I'm not going to give it to anyone else. It's brand-new, so there are no sad memories or history to it. It was for a fresh start for both of us. I thought we needed that." She nodded, and not knowing what else to do, she reached out and took it from him and opened the box. It was a beautiful round diamond solitaire, an engagement ring.

"I don't know what to do with that," she said. "It's beautiful."

"So are you, and you deserve it, Alex," he said softly. "I should have done it sooner. I don't think I even knew how much I loved you until you took care of me after I was shot. I was a mess for a while, but everything you said that day was true. I needed to hear it."

"I haven't heard anything from you for a month," she said, and he nodded.

"I'm not great on that, as we both know. I thought this conversation should happen face-to-face. You're not pregnant?" he asked her gently.

"No, so you don't need to marry me," she said, and handed the box back to him. It was the right thing to do, in her mind, if that was why he was proposing to her.

"That's not why I asked you. I wanted to marry you either way." He didn't take the ring back from her. "Keep it. Can we try again?" he asked, afraid to hope.

"I'm not ready for children yet," she said. "There's a lot I want to do first."

"Me too. But I want to do all of it with you. Nothing means anything without you, Alex. I love you. If you don't love me anymore, I understand, but I wanted you to know. I didn't want to be sorry later that I didn't tell you again. I'm sorry I took so long. I needed to grow up. I wasn't ready when I met you. You changed everything in my life. I want to be here with you, work on the paper, write our books together. Have kids one day if you want them, or not. It's up to you. I love you, whatever you want to do. I want to see the world with you. And live where you are. I fell in love with this place when we spent Christmas here. I'm sorry I never met your grandfather."

"Yeah, me too," she said, still holding the ring box he wouldn't take back.

"I came here because I love you, and I was hoping like hell that you still love me too, even after all the misery I put you through when I got shot."

"I didn't want to lose another person I love. I thought you were going to die. And you might have if you took the job at the paper as head of Crime. I thought they'd kill you."

"So did I. And I don't want to lose you. So . . . what do you think? . . . Is the job still open, or has the position been filled? Or have you decided to run the paper alone?" That was a distinct possibility too, and she was well capable of running *The Beardstown Courier* by herself. He knew that, but he wanted to help. She smiled and handed the box back to him, and he took it as a refusal of his proposal.

"You've got the job," she said. "You're the only one I want to run the paper with. Now do it right." He looked shocked and blank for a minute. He didn't know what she meant. "You know, put it on . . ." She gestured at the box in his hand and the floor with a meaningful look and pointed at his knees, and he laughed.

"Sorry . . . I missed my cue . . ." He got down on one knee in his city suit he wore to important meetings, with the ring in his hand.

"Alexandra Bouvier, will you marry me, to have and to hold, for better or worse, to love and to cherish, and *not* to obey, until death do us part?" She was smiling and she kissed him, still on his knees in her kitchen.

"I'll get back to you on that," she said, as he slipped the bright sparkling ring on her finger, and he stood up and kissed her properly that time. He had arrived a month later than she had, and had taken longer to get there, but he was home now too. It had been a long road for both of them. It was the path that had been meant for them since the day they met. Oliver had been wise enough to realize it before it was too late. Alex smiled as she looked at the ring on her hand and kissed him. It was going to be an interesting life with him. it had taken them two years to get there. They had healed each other's wounds, and were ready to face the future, as equal partners, and Oliver accepted her as the woman he loved, with a mind of her own. And standing together, hand in hand, they made each other brave.

About the Author

DANIELLE STEEL has been hailed as one of the world's bestselling authors, with a billion copies of her novels sold. Her many international bestsellers include *Far From Home, Never Say Never, Trial by Fire, Triangle, Joy, Resurrection, Only the Brave,* and other highly acclaimed novels. She is also the author of *His Bright Light,* the story of her son Nick Traina's life and death; *A Gift of Hope,* a memoir of her work with the homeless; *Expect a Miracle,* a book of her favorite quotations for inspiration and comfort; *Pure Joy,* about the dogs she and her family have loved; and the children's books *Pretty Minnie in Paris* and *Pretty Minnie in Hollywood.*

daniellesteel.com
Facebook.com/DanielleSteelOfficial
Instagram: @officialdaniellesteel

About the Type

This book was set in Charter, a typeface designed in 1987 by Matthew Carter (b. 1937) for Bitstream, Inc., a digital typefoundry that he cofounded in 1981. One of the most influential typographers of our time, Carter designed this versatile font to feature a compact width, squared serifs, and open letterforms. These features give the typeface a fresh, highly legible, and unencumbered appearance.